The Sleepers on the Hill

The first misfortune was that old Miss Cooney fell off her bicycle and had to be taken to hospital. Her neighbours at Ten Cottages tried to keep an eye on her deserted house, but they were put to flight by wasps which had built their nest in one of the ruinous rooms. It was a boy, Tom Connor, who first discovered Kate, Miss Cooney's orphan niece, whom the old lady had kept hidden away. And it was Kate who had found the bangle. She wouldn't say where it came from, but Tom had his suspicions and they increased as more and more trouble came upon the people of Ten Cottages. None of them would have dared even to climb Sleepers' Hill, let alone take anything from the prehistoric graves beneath. But Kate was a stranger . . . .

The Sleepers on the Hill

by

CATHERINE SEFTON

MAMMOTH

First published in Great Britain 1973
by Faber & Faber Ltd
Magnet paperback edition first published 1983
Reissued 1990 by Mammoth
an imprint of Mandarin Paperbacks
Michelin House, 81 Fulham Road, London SW3 6RB

Mandarin is an imprint of the Octopus Publishing Group

ISBN 0 7497 0691 0

A CIP catalogue record for this title
is available from the British Library

Printed in Great Britain
by Cox & Wyman Ltd, Reading, Berkshire

The long men in the shadows
Are silent, grey and still.
They sleep and are forgotten
As they lie upon the hill.

Chapter One

My name is Tom Connor, and this book is about things which happened to the people of the Lanes, not so long ago.

It was summer, almost, and I was eleven. My sister Kathleen was twelve and no better than a nuisance most of the time, telling me what to do . . . or trying to! But I'll say nothing against Kathleen, except that it was more my story than hers, whatever she says. Wasn't it me that went after the egg-thief? Didn't I save us both, when it might have been hard with us? Wasn't it me . . . but I'm stepping in front of myself. The right and proper beginning of this story is the day the fox knocked Miss Cooney off her bicycle.

It was a very old bicycle, all tied together with bits of string, and when the fox ran in front of her Miss Cooney must have thought that her last day had come. She went right, the fox went left, and the bicycle went straight on down the hill toward McArt's bridge. When it reached the bend in the lane the bicycle took no notice, but went straight on over the ditch into the hedge of Hegan's wet field, where I found it.

It was a curious sight that met me, for there was the bicycle upside down in the hedge and a trail of broken eggs leading up the hill, but where was the rider?

All thought of getting the messages home went right out of my head. I dropped the red string bag and started up the hill, quick as I could go. Past Baillie's Field, and the dip by Browbrook's, and there was Miss Cooney, lying in the middle of the lane with the look of a dead one on her, her left leg doubled under her and a slip of hair coming down over her nose, with a paste of blood on it. She was white as an egg, and her breath came in short quick sobs that shook the old clothes she wore.

"Are you dead, Miss Cooney?" I asked her, and if that sounds stupid, it was what came to me to say. If she didn't know whether she was dead or not, who would?

She turned her head to look at me, and gave out a groan.

"Me leg," she said. "Oh . . . oh . . . me leg!"

"Is it broke?"

"The ould fox knocked me off!"

"Can you walk?"

"Me leg! Oh me poor leg!"

She couldn't move herself, I could see that, for she couldn't even sit up properly. I got hold of her and moved her as best I could toward the hedge, just in case there would be a motor-car coming down the lane, though all the time I was wondering whether I would be better to leave her sitting. When a person has broken bones it's better not to move them if you can, in case you make the hurt worse . . . but there she was in the middle of the lane, and there I was, and I knew I'd have

8

to leave her to get help, and from the look of her I knew she needed help quickly. She was eighty if she was a day and she lived all alone in her own house eating next to nothing, and that left her all bone and gristle.

I got her into the hedge and told her to sit tight, then I ran down the hill toward Mrs. Weeney's Post Office, where I had to get Mrs. Weeney out from the pigs to work her telephone and fetch up the ambulance from Darkwater.

We were twenty minutes sitting in the lane with Miss Cooney going on about her leg, waiting for the ambulance to come clanging up. She kept talking all the time, wanting this and that, a cigarette and a cup of tea, and all the time rambling on about people and places I'd never heard tell of.

Mrs. Weeney wrapped her up in two blankets from the house, and stuck a blue boiled sweet in her mouth in place of the cigarette she wanted, for Mrs. Weeney was good-living, and didn't hold with smoking in the house or out of it. I don't think Miss Cooney liked the sweet, for she made a commotion about it, and threw it away, and Mrs. Weeney was cross.

"Is she going to die?" I asked, because there was something frightening about the way she kept talking about nothing, and the funny jumbled-up way she did it. There was a dirty blue bruise on her head where the blood came from, and she looked sick to me.

"You're not to mind her," said Mrs. Weeney, shooing me back. "You're not to mind a word she says, young Tom, for she's nothing but a crazy woman."

"It looks awful bad," I said, peering round Mrs.

Weeney at the old bundle of woman by the hedge, mumbling away to herself. Mind you, everyone knew that Miss Cooney wasn't all there, it was no news to me . . . but it was terrible to see her hurt like that, when she wouldn't lay a finger on a fly.

The ambulance came rocking and bouncing down the lane, knocking the dew off the hedge with its cream and black sides, blue light on top revolving like a lighthouse. There were two men in it and a nurse, and they had Miss Cooney up and inside it in two ticks, moving her so gently that I thought I'd better say nothing about the way I took her off the road. Mrs. Weeney got into the ambulance with her, and that left me to mind the Post Office.

It wasn't the sort of Post Office you'd know about, if you don't live in our sort of country. Mrs. Weeney's Post Office was a lean-to shed tacked on to the back of the house, filled up with lemonade and bootlaces and paraffin and postal orders and stamps and primus stoves and wellington boots . . . but it was a proper Post Office, no doubt about that, and I felt all the grander for being an official temporarily-in-charge Post Master, at eleven years old. I've done the petrol pumps at Maxie Hartnett's in Quinn's Bridge too, many the time.

I sat down in Mrs. Weeney's armchair behind the counter, with the yard cat wound around my feet, and waited for people to come and post letters, but nobody did. That wasn't surprising, for Mrs. Weeney's Post Office was on the way to nowhere, half-way between Ten Cottages and Quinn's Bridge, serving the both of them and the wild men up on the mountain beyond.

There'd be rush days at Weeney's in the summer, with hikers or sea-siders coming with their tents and caravans and postcards down to Gilroy's Point Field, but apart from that there wasn't much business, except on pension day.

The only book in the place was Mrs. Weeney's Bible, which she kept handy by the desk just in case she needed it, and I didn't feel like reading that. So I read a book about family incomes supplement and another about premium bonds and a poster about how to address letters properly to Stowe in Somerset, which is in England where I don't know anybody and wouldn't be sending any letters. Mrs. Weeney's Samuel had two big signs up on the wall which he'd written himself in his own special red ink.

One said

"JOY shall be in HEAVEN over
ONE SINNER that REPENTETH
more than over
NINETY AND NINE JUST PERSONS
which need NO REPENTANCE
ST. LUKE 16: 7"

And the other said

"NO CHEQUES OR CREDIT
BY ORDER
Eileen Weeney (Mrs.) (Prop.)"

I thought that the first one was a bit unfair to all the good people, and wondered if maybe St. Luke or Mrs.

Weeney's Samuel had got it wrong, and the second sign was no better than silly, for it was well known that Mrs. Weeney gave credit to everyone around the Lanes and Ten Cottages, marking it down in her red book . . . maybe the sign was put up for the sea-siders and the hikers, who couldn't be trusted to pay up their bills before they went . . . most probably the bit about Sinners was for them too.

You can't be too careful with sea-siders and hikers. They don't know what they're doing half the time, and go out in boats and lose the oars, or scare the sheep with their dogs, or mistake things for mushrooms, or forget to pay for things. They're very good at forgetting to pay for things, and throwing rubbish out of cars in plastic bags, instead of giving it to the pigs, or burning it on the fire like any sensible person.

I was just getting bored when the telephone bell rang with a terrible jangle, and of course I couldn't find it. There I was chasing the cat around the counter and hunting for the machine in among the gas cylinders and the stamps, till I found it sitting under an egg box with an innocent look on its dial, as if it hadn't been hiding on purpose.

I lifted up the receiver end and said, "Who is that?"

"Post Office?" said the voice inside, back at me.

"This is Tom."

"Who is Tom?"

"Big John Connor's Tom," I said, and then I added, just to let the voice know, "I'm minding the Post Office for Mrs. Weeney."

There was a pause.

"Is that a little boy speaking?" said the voice, testily.

"I'm eleven," I said, not seeing that it was any business of his . . . for the voice belonged to a man, and not a decent countryman either, but a sea-sider by the sound of him.

"I'm making inquiries about cottages," said the voice. "I wondered if anyone at the Post Office could put me in touch with somebody who might know about that sort of thing."

"No," I said.

"Is there anyone else there I could speak to?" asked the voice, sounding impatient.

"No."

"Can you put me through to a . . . I don't know . . . to the Police Station, I suppose."

"No."

"Why not?" the voice demanded.

"I'm only minding the telephone," I said. "I don't work it."

"You'll hear more about this," said the voice, and the telephone went dead.

I went back to my seat, well satisfied. Mrs. Weeney would be pleased with me. All summer we have sea-siders coming looking for cottages, and they are a botheration to everyone. Nobody wants strangers from town knocking about the place. I wasn't a bit worried that the voice was cross because I wouldn't get the Police Station for him. Wasn't I right? There IS no Police Station at Ten Cottages, so of course I was!

When Mrs. Weeney came back I didn't tell her about the phone call, because I didn't think much of it. At the time I was worried about Miss Cooney, not an old seasider on the phone.

"Is she dead?"

"She's alive."

"Will she get better?"

"She'll maybe be no better and no worse than ever she was," said Mrs. Weeney, looking down her nose at me, though I was nearly as big as she was. You could put Mrs. Weeney and her Samuel one on top of the other and they'd still get through the front door without bumping.

"She's not right in the head," I said.

"You're not to talk about that," said Mrs. Weeney, severely. "You'd best be off home, Tom."

Home!

There I was, hours late for home, standing talking to Mrs. Weeney, with the messages . . . *where were the messages?*

They'd been in the red string bag in my hand, coming up the lane . . . then I saw the trail of broken eggs, and found Miss Cooney and . . .

"I'm away off, Mrs. Weeney," I said, hurriedly, and I took off up the lane, to find the bag.

That I could not do! No bag, no messages.

There was supposed to be elastoplast, and lard, and a loaf from Damolly's, and Big John's tobacco, and Kathleen's shoes left off the Darkwater bus at Gilroy's at the Point Field . . . all in the red string bag . . . and the red string bag was as gone as if the sleepers had it on their hill.

I looked everywhere for it, up and down the lane,

without finding so much as a trace, and then there was nothing for it but to go home.

Kathleen was sitting at the table, and she gave me a grin when I came in, as if to say I was for it.

"I didn't mean to lose it," I said, before my mother could get a word in. "I was minding the Post Office. There was an accident. I . . ."

"He's no sense," said Kathleen.

"You're no one to talk," I said.

"Didn't I find it!" she flashed back. "Didn't I find the old bag, where you'd chucked it in the ditch? Didn't I bring it home before the hikers got it?"

"You found it!" I said, all astonishment, and the two of them, my mother and Kathleen, had a laugh at me.

"Well, I don't know at all," I said, sitting down to my potatoes. "Why did nobody tell me it was found?"

"That's enough of your talk," said my mother. "Eat your meal, Tom, for Big John wants to see you out the back, as soon as you've done."

I ate up as fast as I could, not wanting to keep Big John waiting. My father is not a man for waiting, especially when there are things that need doing. As soon as I'd finished I washed my plate and went out over the back wall and across the Harp Field behind the cottages, looking for him. He was down by the old lime burner, gathering up the nets.

Many the time I've come on my father like that, standing by the ruined wall of the lime burner, with the sea beyond him, and his red hair lit up by the sun closing down over the lough. He is a terrible size, and the shape of him in the sunset was like a big burning man.

15

"Is it Tom?" he said.

"It's me."

"I heard Miss Cooney fell off her bicycle," he said.

I told him it was so, and how it came about.

"You may take your sister and see to the hens," he said. "You may look after it for a while, till we see what's to be done about Cooney's."

"Right away," I said, and off I went for Kathleen.

It was like my father to think of Miss Cooney's hens like that, when all that was in my head was wondering if she was dead and fussing about the messages. If Miss Cooney was in hospital someone would have to see to the hens, or the same fox that caused her fall would have a fine dinner. The foxes aren't so bad in summer, for the sea-siders in Gilroy's Point Field and the hikers leave their stuff about and they have fine old feeds without touching the birds, but it is different out of season. If Miss Cooney's hens were to spend the night in the trees or the hedge there'd not be a one left with a skinful of feathers in the morning.

I got Kathleen and we set off crossing the Coastguard's Road and Hegan's Field, then fording the river into Browbrook's River Field and round the side to Cooney's Field, which would bring us to the back of the house itself. That way we would cut off maybe three quarters of a mile, instead of walking down the Coastguard's Road to the bridge and up along Cooney's Lane to the front of the house. It was great gas as a short cut, but mucky.

The sun had gone down, but it was light enough when we dropped over the wall into Cooney's Field, and we could just make out the roof of the house beyond the hump of Sleepers' Hill in the middle, and beyond the house the dark shape of the Mournes rising in the distance. It was getting cold, the sudden way it does in early spring.

"Are you game to go straight across?" I said to Kathleen.

"I am not," she said.

"It's only an ould hill," I said.

But she would have nothing of it, and round the side of the field we had to go, keeping clear of the green hill in the middle, with the gorse wild yellow on the side of it.

"You're scared," I said.

"I'm not daft," she said.

"Mrs. Weeney said it's heathen superstition," I said.

"You don't see Mrs. Weeney on the Hill," said Kathleen. "That's all I'm saying."

We came to the wall round Cooney's House, which was all broken down. My Father told me once the Cooneys were big people, and had land right across the mountain. Now there was only the house and the field left, and the field was hired out to Browbrook, and old Cooney dead and gone in his grave down in Darkwater in their private vault. All that was left was Miss Cooney riding her bicycle and selling her eggs to Mrs. Weeney, or Davie the egg-man from Quinn's Bridge. She got the bicycle off Billy Hanna after the tractor ran over it, and Billy said it shouldn't be allowed back on the road because of the twisted frame . . . but Miss Cooney rode it just the same, for she could afford no better. Don't ask me how or why the Cooneys lost all their money, but lose it they did. I'm only telling how it was in my time.

Anyway, when we came to the big wooden door in the wall round Cooney's house, wasn't it locked.

"There's a thing," said Kathleen, looking at me. "You may climb over, Tom, and open it for me."

I had a mind to tell her she could climb over herself, for I wasn't her footman, but on the other hand I'm a good climber, and Kathleen's just a girl, for all she's older than me, so I shinned up the wall, making the best I could of the handholds on the rough stone, and dropped down on the other side.

It was the oddest ever!

It may once have been a garden, but now there was nothing but a maze of weeds and old tin cans and the back end of an old trap, rotted away and half buried, and the ruin of a tin hut against the wall.

I was glad enough to shoot back the bolt and let Kathleen in, and truth to tell, though she'd never tell it, I think she was glad enough to be back by me.

"Isn't it creepy?" I said.

"You're scared."

"No I'm not."

"Neither am I," said Kathleen, but she said it softly.

Anyway, it was no time for waiting about, for the darkness was almost on us, and I'd not great fancy for finding my way back past Sleepers' Hill in the darkness, superstition or not. So we got through the weeds and the rubbish and opened a rusting gate which let us in at the side of the house, where the gravel was covered in weeds, and the drain pipe had fallen away from the side of the roof, eaten up with rust.

We went round the back and made a quick hand of the hens, till we had the lot of them squawking and complaining their way into the hen-house.

"There's that then," I said, closing over the door. "I'm for home."

But nothing would do Kathleen but she must peer in the windows of the house.

"Come out of that," I said, itching to be away, and wondering what she'd call me if I suggested going back by Cooney's Lane, and not near the Hill at all.

"There's no furniture, Tom," she hissed. "Would you look at that? Not a stick!"

"Aye, well . . ."

"They say she sold it all, and sleeps on a pile of hay."

"I'm going home, Kathleen."

"And you'd hear her talking to herself, if you went past the place at night, and dancing."

"People don't dance with themselves."

"Proper people don't," said Kathleen. "Miss Cooney is mad people."

"She's not mad," I said. "She's just not right in the head."

"Same thing."

"Not lock up mad," I said.

"Aye, well."

"Are you coming home?"

"A minute . . ." she said.

And the next thing I knew, hadn't she turned the handle of the side door, and let herself in.

"Come out of that, Kathleen!" I hissed at her, coming up as close as I dared.

She was half-way down the hall, walking as soft as she could.

"Come out!" I said. "It's not your house."

"Don't be daft!" she said. "Just because you're afraid!"

"I'm not," I said.

"Well then. . . ."

So I had to go in, there was nothing for it, though I didn't like it one bit.

It was dark in the hall, with no light at all, and a funny dry smell. The boards creaked under our feet. I came up beside her, and we stood together at the foot of a staircase leading up to the next floor.

"I dare you," Kathleen said.

"I will if you will," I said, not to be bettered by a girl, even if she was my sister.

We got up as far as the first landing, but we got no further.

"What's that?" said Kathleen.

"What's what?" I said.

Then I heard it . . . and the next minute we were down the stairs, and running for our lives, never caring about who was the braver of the two.

It wasn't till we were safely in the lane and almost at the bridge that we stopped.

"What were you running for?" said Kathleen, casually, as though she hadn't been.

"Same thing as you," I said, trying to get my breath back.

"I was running to catch you," she said.

And that was all she would say.

But she heard the noise as clear as I did, and a queer noise it was . . . like somebody breathing, very very softly, in the dark at the top of the stairs.

I know she heard it, although she wouldn't say so. I know fine well, because that night she went to sleep with her candle lit, for I heard Big John complain about it.

Chapter Two

Cooney's house and the scare we had there went right out of my mind the following morning, when a great excitement happened.

It was the day the letter came for my big brother Willie, telling him he was to go to Aghbo that Sunday, for a county trial.

We were all of us walking on air!

It isn't every family in a place like Ten Cottages or Quinn's Bridge for that matter that has a man picked for a county trial at the football, and I daresay we all felt we had a right to blow about it. The only one who didn't blow was Willie, and he went about the Cottages with a sort of I-told-you-so look on his face, and was out in the Harp Field at the back at midday kicking and catching against Joe Breen in a casual sort of a way, as though he wasn't famous all of a sudden.

Just in case you didn't know, it was proper football Willie was picked for, not soccer football, the English way, or Rugby. Willie was a Gaelic man, and we have our own game. It is something like a cross between the two English games, for there are posts like the Rugby men use, but a net like soccer, and a goalkeeper. It is one point to put the ball over the bar, and three points for a goal in below, and every man on the field can punch and catch the ball as well as kick it. It's the best game there is, of course, and Willie is the best player in all the Lanes, this side of the mountain. My father was a player too and played for the Ten Cottages team when there was one, but now there aren't enough men, and Willie plays for St. Mary's, in Quinn's Bridge.

Needless to say the word went up and down Ten Cottages and the Lanes all in a rush . . . and I did my bit at spreading it. They were all mightily impressed and pleased as well that it was Willie who had to go for a trial and not Turlough McCann from Quinn's Bridge, who is Father Jennet's blue-eyed boy when it comes to the football team, and knows it.

The man who was most pleased by it all was my father, although he tried not to let on. He read the letter four times over, and accidentally took it with him when he went over to Brennans to see about their calf, where he accidentally showed it to Sean Brennan, who was by way of being his best friend. I met him coming back along the beach when I was out for driftwood.

"I suppose we must all be proud of Willie," he said, not able to keep himself away from talking about it.

"Willie's grand," I said.

"He'll need taking down a peg, that he doesn't get too full of himself," said Big John, throwing a bit of driftwood in my sack.

We came by the pier, but there was only the *Marie*

Clare tied up, and no sign of Malachy or Tom Roday who owned her, so we didn't hang about, but kept on toward the cottages.

"I sometimes think, that round here is the most beautiful spot in the whole world," he said, and he kicked away a rusty old beer can as though he'd hardly seen it. It is beautiful, with the mountains running up from the lough in soft granite folds, and the gorse, and the stone heap of the old fort, and the line of the Ten Cottages set against the lip of the tide, and the hulk of the stone pier set out into the water. It is beautiful, though I doubt if it is the most beautiful place in the world . . . but there was no point in arguing with my father about it. People who've been brought up in a bit of land have a feel for it, and there have been Connors at the Ten Cottages and round the Lanes for more years than I know of.

"It is a grand place," he said reflectively. "I don't know why he wants to go."

"Who wants to go?"

"Willie," said my father, with a frown. "He's seventeen now, you understand, and he has big ideas about the town."

I'd heard Willie say as much, but I thought it was jaw, and I'd no idea he'd got as far as telling Big John.

My father looked at the sea and said, "What would you say to that now, Tom?"

I said nothing at all.

"I always thought he'd stop here," Big John said. "But there you are. They have to try their wings. Would you not say so?"

"I'd like to go myself," I said, then I added hurriedly, "Some day, you know . . . when I'm bigger. I'd like to see other places. London . . . like on television. And Belfast."

"Where did you see the television?" he asked, puzzled.

"Mrs. Weeney's Samuel let me see, and there's one at the hotel in Quinn's Bridge," I said. "Willie and me go watching the races and the soccer football."

"Is that so?" he said.

"I wouldn't leave here altogether," I said. "I'd want to come back again, you understand."

"Aye," he said. "I understand. They all say that, Tom."

"Who all?"

"The Sloans. The Conatys."

I knew what he meant.

There are only eight of the Ten Cottages lived in all the year round now, the other two are let to sea-siders, who only come down in the summer. Conaty's and Sloan's are empty in winter, and you pass their dead eyes by, and watch out for the lights of the lamps in the other eight. Ten Cottages all set in a row, and two of them scraped out and prettied up for the bucket-and-spade brigade and the fancy week-enders.

My father didn't say much on the way back to the house, but I understood why. I should never have said about leaving and going to look at other places. He didn't like it, and he liked even less the idea of Willie going . . . I suppose that should have made me jealous, being his son as much as Willie was, but I knew that with Willie it was a matter of now, in the next year or so anyway . . . my time would come.

25

As if to rub salt in the wound, wasn't a sea-sider at Sloan's when we went by it . . . at least there was a big blue car drawn up outside, and a tall man with long shorts bobbing in and out of the door. My father greeted him friendly enough, as is his fashion, but I could see the itch behind it.

Willie wasn't about the house when we got back, and he didn't appear until my father had gone off toward Quinn's Bridge in Davie's van. My father was giving a hand to Jerrerson's on the High Road, where they were painting the barn. It was like that with my father and most of the men in the cottages. They made do with a bit of farming, a bit of fishing and a bit of whatever might be going in the towns by way of an odd job. There was hope that maybe it would change, and Father Jennet was to start a sock factory that would give employment the year round to those who wanted it, but it seemed to be no more than talk . . . and anyway I couldn't see Big John working in a tin shed behind the Parish House, and bending his great rough hands to that finicky woman's stuff.

I was talking to Kathleen in the kitchen about it, when we saw Willie through the doorway. He was coming along the Coastguard's Road from the Point with Mickey Breen. Mickey had his dirty black hat sloped back on his head, and his check shirt open at the neck, beneath the shabby blue pin-stripe jacket he wore, the half of somebody's suit that had seen better days. I had no particular liking for the Breens myself. All eight of them lived in number three, and Mickey and Joe and Brian went up every day to Quinn's Bridge where they worked in Maxie Hartnett's garage, where I minded the pumps one time. I suppose it must have been the day off, for Mickey and Joe Breen to have been at home.

"Hallo, Willie," I said, as the conquering hero came in the door, with his shovel over his shoulder.

There was an air about Willie that day, a real jauntiness, that wasn't just the county team. Maybe it was the going away already growing in his bones, but I didn't want to say anything about that, for I was sure that Kathleen had no word of it, and I thought it had better lie unsaid between us, in case it never happened.

"I know what you never done," Willie said.

"Did," said Kathleen.

"You never done nothing about Cooney's hens this morning," said Willie.

I looked at Kathleen, and she looked at me.

"I thought he was doing it," Kathleen said, getting her word in first.

"Big John will want to know the reason why, that's all I'm saying," said Willie, with a laugh, as he went through to the big room to speak to my mother.

"We'll need to go up there, Kathleen," I said.

She nodded, but she didn't say much about it. Truth to tell neither of us was too happy as we set off for Cooney's. Of course, neither of us was going to admit to being afraid . . . but we had heard *something* there the night before, and the fright was not forgotten.

"How long do you think she'll be in hospital?" I said, thinking about Miss Cooney . . . and, truth to tell, wondering how many visits we would have to pay to the old deserted house.

"Mrs. Breen says they'll lock her away, for she is not right in the head," said Kathleen.

I did not like the sound of that at all, for it is not a good thing to close a person up in a hospital who could be out on their own. I said so to Kathleen. "For all she's daft," I said, "she does no harm to anyone here, riding round on her bicycle with the old clothes falling off her."

"She'd maybe be looked after better in the hospital," said Kathleen. "One time Father Jennet was saying to Big John that Maggie Curran from the Point would be better in the hospital, and Big John said it was so, but you couldn't expect people to shift when they'd been in the one house all their lives and Father Jennet said that was all right, but."

"But what?"

"I don't know but what," said Kathleen, "for Big John caught on that I was listening, and told me it was no business of mine."

"Joe Breen says that Father Jennet wants to change things too much," I said. "He says there will be aeroplanes and helicopters here next, and film stars."

"Do you think there will be?" said Kathleen, brightening up.

"Indeed I do not," I said. "For Willie told him it was a load of nonsense, for what film star would be coming to look round Joe Breen's wee house, and Joe Breen didn't like it and started calling him names, and Willie turned tail and walked off on him."

It was just so too, for that is the way it happened, and Willie said to me that I was to be careful with the

Breens, for they were up to their eyes in their own ditches, and couldn't see the way things were changing all around them. Willie says there will be great changes some day here, and he says that the only man that sees it is Big John, and that the sorrow of it is that Big John has a yearning to keep the place the way it was, and half times is arguing against himself when he tries to tell the likes of the Breens that there should be new things brought in.

We were dragging our feet along the lane, when Kathleen said: "What way shall we go, Tom?"

Now it is not like her to ask such a thing, but I knew what she was at. She wanted me to be the one who would say we should go by road.

"I'm not afraid of Sleepers' Hill, even if you are," I said. "Not in the day-time anyway."

"I'm not afraid of it," she said.

We walked on a bit but, without saying anything to each other, we were going the long way.

"I am a bit afraid of it," I said, for it was the truth, and there was no point in hiding it. "Not because of Dan Breen's stories of fairy lights and such, I don't mean that, it's something about the place."

"I know what you mean," Kathleen said. "It is sort of shivery."

"I asked Big John once, and he said the same. He said old Cooney would not have it touched when he was alive, and that is why the gorse is thick on it now. And Father Bridger in the old times said there was a curse on it, and it a heathen place from the old times, that no man should pass by but he offer up a something to the saints to guide him on the road. And Willie said that that was nonsense, but Big John said there was some truth in it."

"Big John would not say it if it was not so," said Kathleen, as we came over the bridge. We could just about make out the Hill across the fields, though the rough boulder walls almost hid it. In the quiet of day it was hard to think there could be anything mysterious about the place. The sun shone down, and there was a heat haze bothering the air.

"Big John said one time a man from town came by, and told him it was an old gods' place, and that was why the priests did not like it, for they were against the old gods."

"There's only one God," said Kathleen.

"Big John says in olden days people thought there were lots," I said. "Big John says some people still think so, but they are probably wrong, and we must make up our minds when we are big."

"That is not what the priest says," said Kathleen.

But I had had enough of gods, and didn't want to talk about it, so instead I told her what I thought about the noise in the house, which was that it was burglars.

"There's nothing to burgle," Kathleen said.

"Maybe there is treasure in the house, and the burglars heard about Miss Cooney falling off her bicycle and thought they could nip over and pick it up. Then we walked in and disturbed them." I began to wonder who burglars might be. "Joe Dodds went to prison," I said.

"That wasn't for burglaring," said Kathleen. "I mean

burgling. That was for hitting someone with a rock after the dance in Darkwater."

"Just the same," I said, "maybe he was burglaring for a change, after the treasure."

But the more I thought about it, the more unlikely it seemed. For a start Joe Dodds had been away in Liverpool for three months, working on the boats.

"If it wasn't burglars," Kathleen said, "what was it?"

"So you admit you heard something?"

"I'm not saying for sure," she said, carefully, kicking at a stone. "The thing is if I did hear something, what was it I heard, and if I only thought I heard something, what was it I only thought I heard?"

"It sounded to me like somebody breathing," I said.

"If it wasn't burglars," Kathleen said, "it was a ghost."

Now it isn't like Kathleen to admit to even thinking something is a ghost, for many the time she's teased me about being afraid to go along the Coastguard's Road past the Hangman's Barn in the dark.

"You always say there are no ghosts," I said.

"If there are no ghosts, why is the Bible full of them?"

"It isn't."

"It is. Margie Coyle says so."

Well, maybe she was right there. There are all sorts of spirits in the Bible, but then that was in Bible days and today is different. I told her so.

"How different?"

"Modern."

She looked down her nose at me.

We were getting close to Cooney's House now, and the closer we got the slower we went.

We stopped in front of the house, and looked at the curtainless windows. One of them, upstairs and over the front door, had a blanket slung across it.

"That's where she sleeps," Kathleen said. "At least, that's where she would sleep, if she was here. That's where she keeps the hay."

"I bet she has a bed," I said. "That's only talk."

"Prove it."

"I'm not going in there," I said firmly, "and I don't care whether you say I'm scared or not."

We stood looking at the house.

"We'd better go round and see to the hens," Kathleen said.

"You go first, you're oldest."

"You're a boy, you're supposed to be brave."

"We'll both go together," I said.

And we did, half afraid of what we might see, and fearful that some weird thing might jump out at us from the bushes.

Well, we got a surprise, but it wasn't the sort of surprise we'd been expecting at all.

Firstly, the hens were running round the back of the house, instead of still cooped inside.

Secondly, all the eggs were gone.

There wasn't a single solitary one left inside the hen-house.

"Well!" said Kathleen.

"That was no ghost we disturbed!" I said. "That was an egg-thief."

"I bet it was Davie the egg-man," she said.

"And I bet it was an egg-thief-type burglar," I said.

"And what's more I'm going to catch him, so there!"

"You're only a wee boy. You couldn't catch an egg-thief."

"Well . . . maybe not catch him," I said, wishing I hadn't been so hasty. "But I'll find out who he is. Then I'll get the Sergeant from the Barracks in Quinn's Bridge and he'll catch him."

"I bet you won't," she said, scornfully.

"We'll come up tonight and keep watch," I said.

"I won't!" said Kathleen. "I'm not coming up here at night, not for all the eggs in Ireland."

"Scared!"

"Yes. So are you."

Just for once I was going to have one over on her, and show how much braver I was than she was, even though she was a year older. There was no stopping me at that moment.

"I'll come up by myself then," I said. "I'm not afraid of an egg-thief."

"You're not to take Willie, or Big John," she said. "You're to go on your own, if you're so big and brave."

"I don't need any help," I said, grandly. "I can look after myself."

So there it was.

I'd let myself in for waiting round a deserted house in the hope of catching an egg-thief or a burglar, if there was one.

The more I thought about it, the sillier it seemed.

"You said you weren't afraid," Kathleen said. "Now you can just go and prove it, so there!"

Chapter Three

It was about a quarter to nine when I slipped over the wall at Cooney's and dropped down into the thicket in the wild garden on the other side.

I'd taken my time coming across the fields, thinking what a big hero I was, and doing my best to bolster up my nerves. The egg-thief, if an egg-thief there was, would surely want to put the hens in . . . anybody who has ever hunted for eggs in a garden will tell you why. Once I'd spotted him, I'd follow him home, then I'd tell Big John who it was, and he would know what to do. Big John does all that sort of deciding at Ten Cottages, and Willie says he is like an Indian Chief and that it is all wrong, and things should be done properly now that we are modern. But it is no good telling anyone round the Lanes that, for when one of the Breens is up to something or when Joe Heseltine threw Big Annie in the river or when anything happens, it is Big John who sorts it out, and if it is too bad then perhaps someone will tell the priest. It is usually Big John, since Father Jennet came, because our people cannot always understand him with his new ideas. Willie says the people of the Lanes are like savages, with a little local chief in every townland, and I know what he means, but I think there is no harm in it.

I took a bit of a detour coming through the fields, just to steer clear of the Hill. It was one thing to talk about it in the day with Kathleen, and another to go by it alone at night. Mrs. Weeney says it is a heathen superstition and nothing but an old hill, but I was not sure enough. There it was in the moonlight, scattered with yellow gorse, a small crooked tree poking out of one side . . . nothing to be afraid of, and yet I was glad to be past it, and over the wall into Cooney's.

I climbed up into one of the apple trees overlooking the back of the house, and snuggled myself down as best I could. I wasn't sure how long I could wait, for Big John would be angry if I was too late in, and yet I had to give the egg-thief time to appear, or Kathleen would laugh at me, and say I was just a blower.

The hens were still on the loose, most of them nestling in the bushes, but some of them pecking around. They thought they were set for the night.

No egg-thief.

And while we were about it, egg-thief was the word, for I'd stopped Davie on the road when he came by the Ten Cottages that evening, and he swore he'd not seen an egg from Cooney's. He'd been to the house as usual, he said, but there was not an egg left out for him in the usual place, so he'd gone on to Weeney's. Mrs. Weeney told him about the accident, and Davie left it at that.

No burglars.

No ghosts.

The shadows lengthened, and I began to get cold, despite the two sweaters I was wearing. I'd brought my torch, just in case, and every so often I put it under my coat and shone it to check the time by Kathleen's alarm clock, which I'd persuaded her to lend me. Willie has a watch, but you could never get him to part with it. Big John is to get me a watch, if ever he has a good run with the boat again. Big John says the herring are not the same now as they used to be, and it must be the nuclear bombs.

I sat there busy convincing myself that ghosts were Kathleen's imagination, that I'd heard nothing in the house but her breathing, and she'd got scared and I'd run off to keep her company. But crouching in the crook of the apple tree and watching the shadows fall across the yard at the back of the house I couldn't help but wonder.

Suppose there really were ghosts? Suppose there was a ghost in Cooney's? Suppose. . . .

I gave up supposing, and concentrated on watching the house, and not closing my eyes at all, in case the egg-thief would slip by me.

Cooney's wasn't a big house, like the Gaws' house at Darkwater, but it was more than big enough for most people. It was two stories high, and there must have been fifteen or more rooms. It had an orchard, or the remains of one, at one side, and the wild garden I'd come through, and beyond that stabling at the back, though most of it had fallen into rack and ruin. My father said he could remember when they had a trap and three hunters for old Cornelius Cooney and his sons, but that was well before my day. Now the roof had fallen in on the stables, and it wouldn't be all that long before it was off the house as well. The word in Ten Cottages was that Miss Cooney lived in the big room over the front door, the one with the blanket across the window, and that she cooked all alone in the big kitchen downstairs, when she cooked, *if* she cooked. But no-body really knew anything about what she did, for Miss Cooney was not one to encourage callers. There were tales of vans calling at the house years before, and taking away one bit of furniture after another to the sales in Darkwater, but that had come to a stop when there was apparently nothing left to take. There were no curtains on the windows, and here and there there was no glass, but only a piece of cardboard or a slate, rested against the frame from the inside, or a rag stuffed in a broken pane. The back of the house, which was the only part I could see, was mainly what had been the kitchen and servants' quarters . . . and the creepy thing about it was that the back door kept creaking on its hinges.

Naturally enough, when Miss Cooney went down with her eggs to Mrs. Weeney's Post Office she had expected to be coming back in a minute and, in the manner of people round the Lanes, she never bothered to close up behind her. The door sat ajar and, when the wind blew, it moved, creaking on unoiled hinges.

At first I was barely conscious of it, but as time wore on and the big white alarm clock in my pocket showed a quarter to ten, I became more and more conscious of the soft creaking.

The minutes ticked on, and once or twice I had to shift my position to stop cramp setting in . . . no sign of the precious egg-thief.

It was a silly idea anyway, coming out to catch him at night. What did I think I was going to find? After all, while the egg-thief might have been careful enough to come round and herd the hens in, by far the most likely time to find him was the morning, when there would be eggs to steal!

I dropped out of the tree as quietly as I could, which wasn't all that easy, because of my cramped muscles. Then I made my way to the back, and did what I could to flush the hens out of their roosts and into the hen-house . . . taking great care to see that the door of the hen-house was latched, so that there could be no mistake about it. Big John apparently hadn't realized that no eggs had appeared yet from Cooney's, but I was determined that we wouldn't lose another day's supply.

With the door firmly latched and tied with a bit of string, I turned back toward the house. The kitchen door creaked gently, the trees cast dim shadows across the yard, the ivy rustled in the breeze, and the hens clucked their discontent . . . though I don't know what they had to complain about, seeing everything was laid on for their comfort inside.

Home . . . yet I made myself walk across the yard and out through the garden, just to prove that I wasn't giving up too early and running away . . . though Kathleen would surely say so, when I had to tell her that my mission had failed.

I wasn't afraid . . . not *really* afraid, though there was

something about the creaking door and the soft rustle of the grass and the dark shapes of the trees and the blind uncurtained windows on the second floor that would have scared me, if I hadn't been so determined to show that I was brave.

Of course I wasn't scared . . . only Kathleen would be bound to say I was. She'd maybe make out that I never went near Cooney's at all.

And there it was that the stubborn bit of me made me come to a stop.

By rights, I should be home, for the clock showed it was past ten . . . but I wasn't going to have Kathleen laugh at me. I hadn't found the egg-thief, and I'd no explanation for losing the day's eggs. If all I could tell her was that I'd hidden in an apple tree for an hour and a half she was going to laugh me out of the house, and I wouldn't live it down for a month of Sundays.

I had to do something . . . anything . . . so that I could truthfully say I'd done it. Some scaring thing . . . some brave thing, that would mean she could not mock at me.

Something like . . . like what?

The door creaked softly . . . and at the same moment my heart went into my mouth at the very idea.

No.

No . . . but yes! It had to be a "no" thing, or there was nothing brave in doing it. I could have walked twice round the house, or searched the stables or . . . I don't know, something of that sort . . . but there was no doubt about what I ought to do, if I was to convince her that I wasn't scared.

Into Cooney's house . . . again . . . despite the scare we'd already had.

I promised myself that I'd go no more than through the kitchen door, where I'd stand and count to one hundred, then I'd come out again, honour satisfied.

Kathleen couldn't say I was afraid . . . not of the breathing ghost anyway. Nobody could say I was afraid if I was prepared to go back into that dark and empty house in the middle of the night.

Once the idea was firmly in my head I knew that I had to go through with it, even though it was dangerous. Big John had told me often enough not to go near empty houses and the like, for there's always danger in a place like that if you're trapped inside, and nobody knows where you've gone. But I comforted myself with the thought that Kathleen knew where I was and anyway it wasn't a ruin, or a derelict house, though it was the next best thing to it. The ceiling would hardly fall in on me . . . nothing nice and simple like that! Anyway, I wasn't going far in . . . just inside the door.

Nothing to be afraid of.

I found myself in front of the kitchen door.

It creaked gently open, as if to lure me in.

The side door where Kathleen had gone in had let on to the hall of the house, but this one was different altogether. I could see a table . . . so she had some furniture after all . . . but the rest was dark, empty space.

I pushed the door open and stepped inside, on to a stone-flagged floor, with my eyes tightly closed.

Of course, nothing happened.

I opened my eyes. I could see very little. I moved toward the table, and brushed against something, which on inspection turned out to be a chair. There was a plate on the table, as I discovered when I put my hand on it . . . and something else, a sort of big metal ring, like a bangle. I picked it up, and ran it through my fingers. It was heavy, and there were lots of ridges on the sides.

By that time I'd managed to make out the shape of a door. The obvious thing was to open it, to show absolutely and forever that I wasn't afraid. I wasn't going to go through it, that would be too much, but I'd open it, and maybe put a foot inside. That would show her.

Still fingering the bangle, I opened the door. I could see a staircase made of stone, a wooden banister, and what looked like a dustbin.

"There!" I said, out loud, feeling very full of myself. I stepped to the foot of the stairs, and brushed against an old brown coat hanging from a hook on the wall. I counted to a hundred, or rather I began the count, but I never reached the end.

At that moment something terrible happened . . . the alarm clock in my pocket went off!

My heart went out of the top of my head, did a double somersault, bounced off the ceiling, and landed back in my chest, thumping for two. I was out of the house with a stumble and a rush, and every tree was out to get me in the garden as I crashed through them, over the wall at twice the speed of light, and on . . . running . . . till I tripped over my feet and landed face down in the mud of the potato rows, where I lay with my eyes closed and my breath coming in great pants.

I lifted my head.

It was a cold clear night, with a purple sky, and the moon gleaming like a wet stone.

In my hand was the bangle, from Miss Cooney's.

I ought to take it back . . .

I ought . . .

But something odd had come over me.

I don't know . . . I can hardly describe it . . . it was as if the bangle was holding me, not the other way about. It seemed to tighten round my hand. I shook at it, and my hand began to throb. Then my head was throbbing too.

I found myself, with my feet dragging through the mud, crossing the field . . . and then I was by the foot of Sleepers' Hill, and gazing up at the little crooked tree on the side.

I'd come far too far. . . .

I couldn't get rid of the bangle. I couldn't. . . .

Then I was at the foot of the Hill, and starting up it . . . it would be a fine thing if I could tell Kathleen I'd climbed the Hill . . .

A fine thing.

But my head throbbed, and the bangle seemed to twist and slither in my hand and I felt cold and odd and afraid and all of a sudden I set my feet firm and said out loud: "I will not go, God help me."

My legs and feet grew cold, and I felt my whole body shiver, and I felt myself move back . . . right back, down to the bottom, with the bangle loose in my hand.

Without being all that clear how I got there, I found

myself at the edge of the field, looking back at the Hill.

It wasn't very big . . . gorse covered most of it, and there was an outcrop of rock on one side . . . I'd been almost up to the outcrop. *I'd been almost up to the Hill.*

But no one went near the Hill . . . *no one.*

It was the bangle . . . I looked at it in my hand. It was nothing but a bangle.

A part of me said, "throw it away", but another part, a stronger part, argued against. It was not mine. It belonged to Miss Cooney.

I found myself walking round the field, thinking about it. Only a bangle.

Maybe I had imagined the whole thing.

I stood on the boulder wall of Cooney's Field and looked back the way I'd come. I could hardly see the Hill, just the line of it against the sky.

That night, crossing the low fields and fording the river, I felt a quiet sort of fear I have never known before or since. It was as if I had come close to something unknown, and turned away just in time. I kept repeating to myself that it was all right, just a trick of the imagination, that I was not afraid of the Hill, or the bangle. And to prove it I took the old thing out of my pocket and put it on my arm, just to see how it felt. It felt like a bangle . . . just a bangle.

Yet it had felt like something else altogether before. . . . I tried to stop the thought . . . It had felt like a hand, drawing me on.

I was the happy man to see the lamp in the cottage shine out through the curtains, and my mother standing by the door, asking where I thought I'd been to this hour.

And there was a thing. It was gone eleven when I got home . . . and my old alarm had gone off at 10.10 for the alarm setting showed it. I'd been near an hour in Cooney's Field, trying to climb that hill for no reason . . . and it had seemed to me like no more than ten minutes. It was as if I had stepped out of time, if only for a little while.

Luckily enough my father was not about the place, or he would have had something to say about it.

"Your father has been wanting you," said my mother. "Were you up at Cooney's, Tom?"

I nodded my head.

"Your father and the men are going up there to-morrow," she said. "There is supposed to be someone prowling around the place."

"I know," I said.

Chapter Four

The secret of the egg-thief was out!

It was Mrs. Weeney's Samuel, and he wasn't stealing the eggs, but taking them down in his car to O'Neill's in Quinn's Bridge . . . that was what he thought best to do, for he knew she'd be needing the money, and he had to go in there anyway.

But it wasn't the egg-thief who brought the men from the Ten Cottages (including Willie and myself) out into the Harp Field at five o'clock the next morning. It was what Mrs. Weeney's Samuel had seen . . . a face at one of the windows.

Of course, the whole story of my adventure with Kathleen, and our breathing "ghost" came out all in a tumble. In retrospect Kathleen began to play a bigger and more important part than I remembered, for the way she told it she was checking the doors to see that no burglars could get in, and only ran away because I ran . . . but there it was. Someone was skulking about the house, and we were to sort it out between ourselves, the way that sort of thing is always done when it's just amongst the Lanes.

"Time enough for the police if it's a stranger," said my father. "Who'd bring the Sergeant in if it is one of our own?" and I suppose he was right.

After all, Mrs. Weeney's Samuel might have seen Kathleen and me go in, and we'd have been mighty annoyed if the entire Quinn's Bridge Police Force had arrived panting on the door, all three of them. If someone from the Lanes or the mountainside was the culprit, wouldn't they be better looked after by the men from Ten Cottages, and given the sort of scare that would keep them out of trouble in future?

"It'll be one of the Rooneys from above, maybe," my father said. "Or some of the men from the caravans at Point Field, the same as broke the windows at Gilroy's last year."

All the men had their own candidates except Willie, who seemed to have little taste for the business. He had said his piece about getting the Sergeant and got short shrift for it . . . indeed bad looks and mutterings from Mickey Breen, who played his part with the mouth before we set out, although he couldn't be persuaded to come with us. Mickey Breen and the Sergeant were old enemies, in particular over the bullock of Joe Henry's that went over the right of way across Harry Siddon's field . . . but that's another longer story, and Mickey got fined £10 and bound over, for all he said the bullock bit him first. As my father said, if the bullock bit Mickey Breen he wasn't over-choosy about his feed.

My father stood by and listened to the talk about what we should do. Sean Brennan had come down from the farm, and there was Joe Coyle and Dan Breen the soft-headed one and Peter Watson and Willie and me, though Willie got that cross that I thought he might chuck it in.

They made that much noise arguing amongst themselves that the holiday-maker in Sloan's got up, and we saw his pale face at the window, peering out to see if the French had landed.

"Big John wouldn't do it, if there was going to be trouble, Willie," I said, talking to him at one side from the crowd, for he'd drawn back with one of his moods on him.

"And what about him?" said Willie, pointing at Joe Coyle. We'd started up the path from the Harp Field that would take us across the Coastguard's Road and into Hegan's where we'd strike across the ford . . . a route I'd taken the night before with all hell's demons at my heels. Joe Coyle was leading the way, with his shot-gun tucked under his arm. I don't think my father was happy about the shot-gun, for I saw him frown and whisper something to Joe, and they walked apart from the rest of us for a little while. I couldn't see what happened, but I have a notion that Big John was trying to persuade him to unload it, at least he came away from Joe's side looking satisfied with his work.

It was a bright and clear morning, nippy. Willie was rumpled up in his donkey coat, and looking bigger and more of a man than I'd ever seen him before.

"Isn't it always done this way round here?" I said.

"I've no liking for setting upon people in the Lanes," he said. "It is no way to go about things."

"Why not?"

"Because there are police for this sort of thing. The old days are gone. Time was when any quarrel in the country could be settled by the fist. . . ."

"And right enough too."

"For the man with the fist. Not right enough for the man on the end. Don't you mind the row about Danny Trim's hedge, and the beating he got last Hallowe'en? And how about your man McClean, the Protestant, and the men who had him in the barn and knocked his teeth in? That is the country way of settling an argument, and it works well enough when there's someone like Big John along, to see it comes to no more than a scaring . . . but it isn't always somebody like him, and people like Mickey Breen are not to be trusted at it."

"But Big John is here, there'll be no bad blows thrown this day . . . just a shaking up, to scare the prowler off."

"I hope so," said Willie.

But all his foreboding couldn't put me off. Truth to tell I felt very manly, finding my way across the fields with the men. I was out of my bed, and armed with a stout stick, and there was Kathleen left behind, despite all her talk about being bigger than me, and told not to stir after us, or my father would see to her. Oh it was men's work, indeed it was, and I'd taken my place along with the rest.

Just the same, Willie had a point. Joe Coyle was not a man I'd trust far, and big Dan Breen, for all his gormlessness, was a strong brute of a man. If the prowler were to cross Dan Breen, he'd likely find his brains scattered over the garden. Coyle wasn't the fighting type, but he had a dandy fine temper . . . it is the thin wiry ones that cause most of the trouble, Big John says, for they know they have to hit first when it comes to fighting, and there is no knowing what that can lead to. The other side of the argument was that a man with a small farm or a boat to depend on, and maybe four or five mouths to feed, would be in a hard way if the Sergeant sent him to prison. I've known those around the Lanes who would have it that they'd prefer a beating any day to going up before the court . . . and the court is what it comes to, if you call in the Sergeant.

We came across Browbrook's Field and over the wall in Cooney's Field . . . and there was the Hill again. I made myself look at it, and at the same time my hand went to my pocket, where the old bangle was still.

I'd not told a soul about it. I don't really know why . . . well, maybe I do now, but I didn't then. It was a daft thing, for I'd had a look at the bangle under the bed-clothes, and it was no more than an old bit of jewellery, a dark thick thing like a fancy curtain ring, with a raised pattern round the side, like the swirls on an Irish dancing cape. There was nothing sinister about it at all. Truth to tell I felt a bit silly, as if I'd been making up stories, when all that had really happened was that I'd lost my way in the dark and got scared . . . but it *wasn't* dark, and I *hadn't* lost my way.

The general notion was that we would dash in and catch the prowler with his trousers down, before he was properly awake . . . then there would be no need for a fight or trouble. My father thought it was probably the best thing to do it that way, and so did Sean Brennan and Willie . . . "If we've got to do it at all," was how Willie put it.

Joe Coyle wanted to go battering on the door, in the hope that our man would come out. Then we could jump him. But my father ruled it out, on the grounds that the prowler had stood his ground when Kathleen and I went in, and we would lose the benefit of surprise if we banged.

The argument came to an end, and we were to go my father's way.

As the man who's been inside the house and knew his way about I had my moment of glory, for I was put to the front to be leader, and I may say I felt very grand. Willie and Big John came just behind, in case I should find myself in trouble, with Joe and Dan and Peter Watson all in a group, and Sean Brennan bringing up the rear . . . for although Sean is not a big man like my father he has his wits about him, and would know what to do if things went wrong. Joe Coyle was fed up about it, and saying it was no way to run a fight at all . . . and my father had to shut him up, and say there would be no fighting if we could avoid it.

In no time at all, and coming as quietly as we could, we were over the outer wall, across the wild garden, and on to the gravel at the side of the house. I pointed out the door Kathleen had gone through, and Big John, Peter and Sean went that way, then I took Willie and Dan and Joe round the back to the kitchen, and showed them the other way in.

"Stay where you are, Tom," said Willie, and he would have none of my protests.

So I was left on guard in the kitchen, and truth to tell that was scaring enough, once all of them had disappeared into the house. I could hear them walking about on the bare boards, and all the time I was waiting for the sound of a rumpus. The house was a creaky sort, and Dan Breen and my father were great heavy men not given to fairy footsteps.

I had half a mind to put the bangle back where I'd found it, now that I was on my own. I took it out and had another look at it, but I didn't put it down. It might be valuable, after all, and the house was empty, with some dishonest person going round it. The bangle must be some old funny thing of Miss Cooney's, and it was up to me to keep it for her, now that I'd found it. I was standing fingering it, and wondering about the design on the side, when there was a roar, and a bang, and the next moment a terrible yowl came from somewhere upstairs, and something landed on the kitchen roof, tumbled and rumbled down it, and Joe Coyle fell flat on his face on the soft grass outside. He was up as soon as he was down, and set off for the hills yelling blue murder.

I wasn't over that amazement before Big Dan Breen broke into the kitchen, cursing and screaming and tearing at his hair, and close behind him came my father and Sean Brennan. Last of all was Willie, who had his jacket pulled over his head, and was laughing fit to bust.

"Out, Tom!" he shouted. "Out quick, before they get you!"

"What?"

"Wasps!" said Willie. "Joe Coyle put a shot through

a wasps' nest in the room upstairs, and they're out for their own back."

The next minute I heard them, dive-bombing down the stairs . . . and off I set, dodging and weaving into the long grass, and making hell for leather for the wall, with Willie beside me.

The others were standing in Cooney's Field, counting their stings.

It was well for Willie he could laugh, for I could see Joe Coyle's arm, and it was stung to a terrible size . . . and my father had a nasty bulge on the side of his face. Poor Dan Breen had got the worst of it, because he was nearest the nest when Joe Coyle took his pot shot, and not as quick as Joe, who headed for the window as soon as he realized what he had done. I think my father was wild with Joe, who'd obviously been intent on making a big noise that would scare the prowler out . . . only he fired his shot in the wrong room, not expecting there'd be a wasps' nest inside a house.

"I've never seen such a place," said Sean. "Nothing but bare boards on the floor, and not enough in it to furnish a room, let alone a house. Half of it eaten away with rot . . . and wasps in a house is a new one to me."

"Who'd have wasps in their house anyway?" I said.

"An old woman who couldn't clear them out by herself, that's who," said Big John. "I doubt if she's been in that room for years . . . the door was closed up, and I suppose as far as she was concerned it might as well have been out of doors, for there wasn't a pane of glass left in the place."

"The laugh is on us," said Joe ruefully. "Grown men chased by a pack of wasps."

Then there was nothing for it but they must start back across the fields to Ten Cottages to get their stings seen to, for truth to tell Joe and my father and Dan were not a pretty sight.

"Coming, Tom?" said Willie.

"I'll maybe stay," I said.

"Suit yourself," he said.

I waited till they had gone, then I went back into the wild garden and stood there for a moment, looking round me.

"Are you there, Kathleen?" I said, for I was absolute certain sure she was, despite being told not to come.

"You are there," I said. "Come out now, for Big John is back for the Cottages, and if you're not back before him you'll get skelped."

Not a sound from her.

Maybe she was hiding round the side of the house.

I made my way back and round to the kitchen door, which was flapping open.

"Kathleen!"

Not a word.

"Kathleen! Kathleen!"

The door creaked behind me, and I whirled round.

"Don't play silly games, Kathleen, this is important."

The door moved again . . . and it wasn't the wind.

"Come out of that," I said. "I know you're hiding behind the door."

The door moved slightly, and someone stepped out from behind it.

It wasn't Kathleen. It wasn't a hiker, or a sea-sider.

It was a small black-haired girl with a dirty face, and she was pointing Joe Coyle's shot-gun straight at my chest.

Chapter Five

We stood looking at each other, and for a long moment nobody said anything.

She was first to speak.

"Go away," she said, and she wagged the shot-gun at me.

It was a double-loader. I knew Joe Coyle had fired it at the wasps' nest, but had he fired both barrels?

"I'm going," I said, for it was no time for messing about. She was small enough, and she didn't look very old, maybe not more than nine or ten, but she was certainly old enough to point the gun in the right direction and fire it, if she wanted to. I was in no mood to get myself shot.

"Go on then," she said. "And don't come back. I don't want you here."

"Why not?"

"Go away."

"All right," I said, but something held me where I was. She looked scared, and a bit sleepy, as though she'd been wakened up by all the noise we'd been making.

She wore a tartan frock and big black farming boots, no socks, and a green sweater with a white peacock design, although the peacock was very mucky. Her hands and face were dirty, and her long hair kept falling over her eyes.

"Who are you?" I said.

"Who are you?" she countered.

"Big John Connor's Tom," I said.

"How did you know my name?" she asked.

That took me aback. I didn't know her name. I had no idea who she was . . . then I realized what had happened.

"Kathleen?" I said.

"Kate."

"I didn't know your name," I said.

"You were calling it," she said, raising the gun a little, and looking suspicious. "You did just know my name, and if you tell me lies I'll shoot you. Go away."

"It's my sister's name," I said. "Kathleen is."

She still looked suspicious. Then she said: "That girl that was in the house? The one with the pretty hair?"

Well, I'd never thought of Kathleen's old hair as pretty, for it was fair and not red like mine and Willie's and Big John's . . . I suppose she got it from my mother's side of the family, for they were Skillens from the mountain, and they all had fair hair, and my father said they were the Dana, or the golden people, the same as in the old books about Ireland.

"That's right," I said. "Was it you. . . ?"

"You'd no right in our house," she said.

"Your house?"

56

"I'll tell my auntie," she said.

I scratched my head in bewilderment.

"Miss Cooney?" I said.

"Auntie Cooney," she said.

"You live here?"

She nodded.

"But nobody lives here except herself. Sure anybody knows that. You can't live here, we'd have seen you."

"Well I do. I'll tell Auntie Cooney when she gets back."

"She had an accident," I said. "She fell off her bicycle. She had to go to hospital."

"I don't believe you."

"Where is she then?"

"Those men took her away," said the girl, raising the gun again, for she had allowed it to dip while we were talking. "She said they'd come and take her away, and I wasn't to let them take me. And I'm not. So you can just go away, all of you."

"Nobody is going to take you away," I said. "But you can't stay here."

"I am staying here, just," she said, and she almost shouted it at me, and waved the gun. "I'll shoot anybody that tries to take me away, that's what I'll do. And if you don't want to get shot you won't come again with your men looking for me."

"They weren't looking for you . . . well, not you exactly. They thought there was a prowler in the house."

"You'd no place coming in our house," said the girl.

"Miss Cooney is very sick," I said. "We came up to look for the hens. Then you saw us, and later on

Samuel saw you, and that's why the men came. They were only trying to look after Miss Cooney's house for her!"

"Will she die?" the girl asked.

"She'll be all right," I said, for the way she looked at me I could see she was scared . . . goodness knows what kind of a time she'd had. It must have been very frightening for her, staying in the house all alone, not knowing where Miss Cooney had got to.

"When did you come here?" I asked.

"That's none of your business," she replied, wrinkling her nose.

"Don't you ever go out?"

"My auntie doesn't like me going out, only when she says."

"I haven't seen you."

"I don't let people see me. My auntie says I'm not to. So you just go away."

"But you can't stay here on your own."

"I can just."

"My father won't let you," I said. "He'll let you come to our house, till your auntie is better."

"I'm not going to anybody's house," she said. "I am not indeed. And you're not to go telling anybody I'm here, John Connor's Tom, d'you hear? I'll shoot you if you do."

"But you can't . . ."

"I can just. I can stay here as long as I like. And you'll promise not to say a word to anyone, or I'll shoot you this minute."

She took a firm grip on the gun.

"You shouldn't point that at people," I said. "It is dangerous. It might go off."

"I might fire it off if I'd a mind too," she said. "But I won't, if you promise."

There was nothing else I could do, so I said: "Okay, I promise."

She didn't lower the gun. "And you'll give back what you took," she said.

"I didn't take anything," I said . . . then I remembered the bangle. "Oh, oh yes," I said, not a bit sorry to be rid of it anyway. "I was looking after it for Miss Cooney." I pulled it out and handed it to her.

"It isn't hers," she said. "And you took it."

"I didn't," I said. "And I didn't know it was yours."

"It isn't," she said, "not exactly. I sort of found it somewhere."

"I wish you'd stop pointing the gun," I said, not really caring very much about the old bangle, now I was rid of it.

"You'll not let on to your daddy that I'm here?"

I shook my head.

"You'll promise to be my true friend and help me hide?"

"Yes."

Then she did a strange thing. She smiled at me, and she held the gun out to me. "Go on," she said, "you take it."

I took it quickly, before she could change her mind. I checked it, and put the safety lock on.

"You're to stop people coming here," she said. "Do you hear me now? You're my promised friend, and

59

you're not to let people come here till my Auntie Cooney comes."

"She's sick in hospital."

The girl shook her head. "No."

"I can prove it."

"How?"

"I'll get Kathleen. She's older than me. She'll tell you it's true."

"You said you wouldn't tell people."

"Kathleen isn't people. She's my sister. She isn't grown up, anyway."

"She might tell."

"She won't," I said. "I'll make her promise."

"Well. . . ."

"We could bring you up some food," I said. "Apples and . . . and things like that. Whatever you like."

"What sort of things?"

"Well . . . lemonade, from Weeney's."

"And a loaf."

"If you like."

"And jam."

"All right."

"And you won't tell anybody else?"

"Not a soul."

"Cross your heart?"

"I've already crossed my heart."

"Do it again."

So I did it again.

She got up from the step. She was much smaller than me, and brown-eyed. She looked very pale and thin, but there was a tough thing about her as well.

"What age are you?" I asked.

"Eleven," she said.

"When?"

"November."

"Oh."

She might look younger than me, but she was older. I was eleven in December, so she had me by one month. It was funny because she didn't look that old at all.

"When are you coming?" she said.

"As soon as I can," I said.

She shook her head. "No."

"Why not?"

"You must come at the same time as last night, when nobody will see you."

"But that's ages and ages from now . . ."

"You promised not to give me away," she said.

"I know but . . ."

"You promised."

And that was that.

Chapter Six

When I got back to Ten Cottages, all full of my adventure, it was to find that Kathleen and my mother and father had all gone to Quinn's Bridge in Ossie Convery's van, for Kathleen was to have a new dress, and my father had business to attend to with Father Jennet, who had sent word with Pat Byrne the Insurance man when he came with his weekly book.

So there I was, left at a loose end. Willie took himself off with Frank McCarroll to the boat shed beyond the Coastguard cottages, telling me sternly to see to it that the range was kept banked up for mother, who would need it hot for our dinners.

Truth to tell, my nose was put out, for I had expected to have a long talk with Kathleen about Kate Cooney, and how we could persuade her that she couldn't stay alone at the house till her aunt came out of hospital . . . if ever she did. It must have been a strange life for Kate, living up there all alone with old Miss Cooney, and never being allowed out when she might be seen at all. I wondered how long she had been there, with none of us knowing or guessing. Nobody ever went to Miss Cooney's except Davie the egg-man, so I suppose it wasn't that surprising. We might never have found out about her, if it hadn't been for Miss Cooney and the fox. Then Kathleen and I and Mrs. Weeney's Samuel and Davie the egg-man were all up at the house, followed by the special catch-the-prowler party . . . altogether more visitors than Miss Cooney's house had had in the last five years.

There were other intriguing things about the girl. What did she do about school? She didn't go to Quinn's Bridge, or Master Hewitsons, I knew that, for we would surely have had word of her if she had. Perhaps she went away to school like children in books, and only came home for the holidays . . . or perhaps she was never sent to school at all, but kept at home, so that her life was one great big long holiday?

I went down to the beach in front of our house, and started throwing sticks for Dessie Owen's dog, Whitey. Dessie came down from the pier and hailed me.

"Did you see your man's wee tricycle affair?" he said.

I shook my head.

"Him that is in Sloan's. The Professor from town with the funny pants. He has a tricycle . . . d'you not see it up there by the cottage?"

Then he took me up from the sands, and right enough there it was, shining blue, a great big tricycle, like a baby would ride, and not what you'd expect to see a grown man on.

"It'll be some new fashion at the University," I said. "Willie was telling me they get up to some odd things

63

there, that you'd never hear tell of with sensible people."

"Is it for the fairies to ride around on, or what?" said Dessie with a sneer.

I was embarrassed, for I feared the man would hear us, as we were right outside the front door of Sloan's. It is a difficult thing to explain to someone who doesn't live at a place like Ten Cottages, but the way people go on there isn't meant to be unpleasant or inhospitable, it just seems that way to outsiders. Joe Coyle, and Dessie, and the Breens in particular could be very awkward with a stranger, just because he was a stranger in their bit of land. Come to that they could be very awkward with their own neighbours . . . but it was more than just the likes of them. Me and Willie, Big John, Sean Brennan . . . we're ordinary enough people, and give offence to no man, but we hold to our own, and we hold that if people don't like our own, why, they needn't come near us, and can stay in their cities. I heard in the school there are people in towns who don't know their own, and never pass a word with their neighbour, but would say our way is nasty and inhospitable. Well, as I see it, our way is our way, and we sort all right with each other, and the other people come and go like flies in the summer, and we pay no more heed to them than we have to, as long as they don't interfere. If they do, it is a very different story.

What I am trying to say is that you mustn't think too hard of Dessie and the Breens and the like, for holding to their own. In a place like Ten Cottages, aren't your own all you've got?

"Come away from that, Dessie," I said. "Isn't the

64

man a sea-sider, and would know no better than to bring a fairy cycle here, when anyone could tell him our hills would be too much for it."

Just then what I had been afraid of happened. The sea-sider appeared in the door of Sloan's, and smiled at us, taking off his dark sun-glasses, and polishing them on the side of his bright red shirt.

"Good afternoon to you boys," he said.

Dessie didn't like that, and he gave me a sideways gleek, and turned round to face the new man. "Afternoon, sir," said Dessie, with a careful little smile, showing his big teeth. "I was admiring this vehicle of your'n."

"Very handy, don't you think?" said the man. "Very easy to get around on in the traffic, once you have the knack of it."

"Oh this is a terrible place for the traffic," said Dessie, sounding very serious. "Doesn't the bus come once a day?"

I don't think the stranger knew what to make of Dessie, for he frowned, and popped his glasses back on his long nose.

"Come away, Dessie," I hissed.

"Maybe," said Dessie, getting more and more pleased with himself, "maybe it'll grow up to be a big bicycle one day."

And he put out his hand, and rang the little silver bell on the handlebars.

"Maybe you should feed it oats," he said. "Just the job for a wee tin critter like that."

The sea-sider turned on his heel, and closed the door firmly behind him.

Dessie gave a great laugh, like a hee-haw donkey.

"That was a bad day's work, Dessie," I said.

"Sea-siders!" said Dessie with a sneer.

I had a notion that the man in Sloan's might hear more of Dessie, and I wasn't wrong. An hour later I saw him talking to Mickey Breen, and by midday, when I was out digging the spuds in the back, I spotted their game.

There was the tricycle, popped up on the roof of the tin kitchen at Sloan's.

It was badness, no more and no less, and I didn't like it one bit, for the new man would go back to his town and tell the world that all at Ten Cottages were ill-bred and no better than the people in the caravans on the Point, with their washing and their motor bikes and their plastic bags of rubbish.

Well, I wasn't going to let it stand like that, even if it annoyed the Breens and Dessie Owen. I put down my spade, and walked along the back of the cottages, till I was almost level with Sloan's, keeping into the wall so that I would not be seen.

It was an easy enough job then to hop up on the rain barrel, and climb from there on to the low tin roof, and walk along it.

That was easy enough, but when I stepped out on to the flat roof of the kitchen, I made a noise like thunder, and the next thing I heard was his footsteps coming to the door.

Down I went on my chest, hoping that he wouldn't be able to see me.

I heard the door open, and I put my cheek down against the tin.

There was a moment's pause, the scrape of a chair,

and a pair of sun-glasses attached to a beaky nose appeared over the lip of the roof.

Two white eyebrows shot up in surprise.

I looked at him, and he looked at me.

I let go of the tricycle.

It rolled slowly down the roof, and fell off.

"Charming!" he said.

"I . . . I . . . ."

"You didn't put it up there, I know," he said. "But you certainly let it fall off!"

"Sorry," I stammered.

He got down off the chair he was standing on, and righted the tricycle. After a moment or two examining it, he turned back to me. By that time I had jumped down from the roof of the cottage and was standing by, looking a bit shame-faced.

"I . . . I . . . ."

"Say no more!" he said, holding up his hand to stop me. "Not your fault. I think I know who it was. Curious example of the local temperament. One lives and learns. I shall take note!"

"We're not all like that," I said. "You're a stranger, and I wouldn't have you thinking that the people from the Ten Cottages are all like Dessie. For indeed we are not, and I'll tell my father and he will speak to Dessie, and the Breens, now see if he won't."

"Ah!" he said. "Now I have you placed. You belong to the big man with the red hair in the end cottage, do you not? Mr. Connor, I think."

"Tom Connor is my name," I said, proudly. "Big John is my father."

67

"He has been most helpful," he said. "Showing me the pump, you know, and giving me some information about tide levels I required. Unlike your other friend, as you so rightly say."

"My father welcomes all here, if they do us no harm," I said.

"Harm!" he said, musing. "There's a word! What would you call harm, young Tom?"

"I haven't thought about it," I said. "Things like they do, I suppose, the people on the Point."

"Mr. Gilroy's caravan camp? You don't approve of that then?"

"Indeed I do not," I said. "They are noisy people, and they scare Dan Breen's cows, and yell and shout and spread themselves all over the fields, as if they owned us all."

"You resent the intrusion?"

"Indeed we do!"

"Well now . . . I'm sure I'm most obliged to you for the information," he said. "You must tell me more about the Ten Cottages, Tom Connor."

"I'll tell what I can, sir," I said.

Indeed I could have told him that it wasn't only the people from the caravans we could do without, but strangers in our cottages as well, though I knew it was not a thing my father would have me say, for the sake of politeness.

"Well, John Connor's Tom," he said, taking off his glasses again, and absent-mindedly cleaning them on his shirt, "you must come inside, and break bread with me."

Then he took me inside, and as good as his word he

brewed tea on Sloan's old black range, and toasted some toast by the flame, which he then spread with a black stuff from a jar, the like of which I have not had before.

"It is a curious jam, sir," I said, by way of conversation.

He laughed at that, and told me the name for it, caviare.

"It is not a bad taste," I said, thinking myself that it was fishlike, and not what I would choose. He then told me a thing that is hardly true, that it cost pounds in money just for a jar, and that it was held to be a special delicacy.

Truth to tell I did not like it, and I doubt he was having a joke with me. What man would pay pounds for a black fish thing like that, when there are herring to be had in the sea, and fresh crabs, and all there for the taking, with no pounds at all to pay? If it had been Kathleen I'm sure she would have tossed it down and had none of it, but I know my manners where strangers are concerned.

"Now, young Tom," he said. "I have some questions for you."

And he took out a great black notebook, and a shiny golden pen, and began to ask me all manner of things about the fishing, and the soil, and what manner of place Ten Cottages was, and where we had our water and all manner of other things, till I had had enough, and made excuses that I must be on my way.

He thanked me politely, and showed me out, and I was glad to be free of him.

The next great excitement was the fight between

Malachy from the *Marie Clare* and the four boys from the caravans, and truth to tell I knew little of it, for all I had in the telling was what Willie knew, and he did not come on the scene until the end, though he paid dearly for his pains.

It seems that Malachy came down to the pier at midday to cast off, to find four of the caravan boys standing on his deck, and larking around with a lobster pot. He'd no sooner given them his mind about it . . . and may a man not give his mind on his own boat . . . when the biggest, a great heavy brute they called Jimmy, picked up a stone and threw it at him.

Now Malachy Byrne is not the easiest of men, and he started after this boy along the beach, and caught up with him, and would have taught him a thing or two, but that the other three intervened. When he saw how things were going Malachy gave a great bull whoop, knowing full well that he would be heard by those who would know what it meant.

The first man to him . . . not surprisingly . . . was Dan Breen, never minding the bandages all over him and the after-effects of his wasp sting. Dan Breen would put the fear of God into anyone he is so big, and he set two of them aside, one to each hand, while Malachy did what he could with the others. To make a short story of it, Dan and Malachy put them to their heels, and the four of them were making off toward the camp when Willie came running down the road from the Coastguards, having heard Malachy yell . . . it was not the first nor the last time that the men from the cottages have had a sort out with the sea-siders from the caravans, and

Willie sized it up at a glance. He came straight into the path of the first of them, a fellow called Dick Spence, with a bushy moustache, and this one, who was not a man to take a straight fight, raised a rock and tossed it at Willie, catching him a hard knock on the side of his head, and laying him stone cold in the road.

It was not the best way to be training for a match, but when Willie came round it was himself he took to cursing.

"It wasn't your fault," I said, helping him back into the house.

"It is the fault of this whole place," he said. "For we live as if we were in another age."

I pointed out that the strangers attacked Malachy, not the other way about.

"I'll soon be out of it," he muttered. "I'll not stay here fighting and feuding over a scrap of ground or a right of way or a few lobster pots."

I had him set on the sofa in the front room when the others came in, full of talk of the journey to Quinn's Bridge, and the new clothes Kathleen had bought. When my mother saw Willie the blood drained from her face, and she was all over him, inspecting the lump on his head, and declaring that now he could never play in the football match.

"Indeed I will!" said Willie, sitting up, and looking suddenly so much better. "Won't I?" he said, appealing to Big John.

But Big John said nothing.

He sat by the range poking at it with the short poker, a flush across his cheeks and his jaw set, and not a word did we have out of him, despite the pirouetting of Kathleen in the new dress. Being the only girl, Kathleen is by way of a favourite, and when she has herself dressed nicely for church or some other place my father is like to be all over her, but there was none of that this time, and Kathleen was sorely vexed.

"It is whatever word Father Jennet had with him," she said, when we were setting the table. "I don't know what it was, but his back is badly up for sure."

And so it seemed to be.

There were some around who said that Big John was soft on us, since the other John died. That was my other brother, and the reason for my father being Big John, for my brother was his first son, a year older than Willie. He was little John, till he didn't come home with the boat that night, and the next week wasn't he floating in Geery Bay. Since that time Big John seemed to take more count on the rest of us, in the manner of a Ten Cottages man . . . though it might seem harsh to an outsider. But he talked to us, and told us what he could of things . . . never mind that Willie said he had it wrong, nearly every word he said. . . .

That night, he would say nothing, but went out after his tea to Brennan's, with no more than a grunt to anyone.

It wasn't till he had gone that I could get Kathleen on her own and tell her the story I was bursting to tell about Kate Cooney at the big house.

"It's a joke!" she said. "Are you wise? To think I'd believe a tale like that?"

"Oh, and is that a joke then?" I said, pulling the string

bag out from under the bed, and showing her the jam and bread I'd got to take with me to Cooney's that night. "You'll not deny that that is food right enough, will you? And what would I be buying bread and jam for, if not for Kate Cooney?"

"Well. . . ."

"And you are to come with me, Kathleen," I said. "For I've told her the aunt is in hospital, but she will not heed me. Between us we must tell her not to stay in that house, but to come out where she can get decent meals and a bed, till we find what is to be done."

At that Kathleen's face lit up. "She must come here," she cried. "Won't that be someone to talk with?"

"You talk to me," I said.

"I'm not interested in your football," she said. "That's for you and Willie."

"Well, at least you believe me," I said.

She said she didn't know what she believed. "The proof will be when we go to the house," she said, and I was agreeable to that, for I knew I would be proved right.

"We're for a walk," I said, innocently, about twenty past eight.

"Not like last night," said my mother automatically.

"I'll go with him," said Kathleen, standing up. "I'll keep him out of trouble!"

She could not resist the least chance to show that she was the bossy older one, and that I was too young to be bothered with. But I let her off with it, for what was the point in making the fuss, when there was the excitement of smuggling the string bag with the food out, and

73

meeting Kate Cooney secretly in the deserted house.

We managed the food easily enough, for I went out first, and Kathleen handed the bag through the back window. Once we were clear of the Harp Field we reckoned we were safe, otherwise excuses about having a moonlit picnic were going to sound very thin. However, we made it that far without mishap, though Pat Byrne the Insurance man nearly caught us in the glare of his headlamps as he drove by.

"The Lanes," I said.

"Why not across the fields?" Kathleen asked.

"Too mucky," I said, for I didn't want to tell her about Sleepers' Hill, and what happened to me there. One tall-sounding story was enough for one day, and I was beginning to worry, in case something would go wrong . . . for wouldn't I look foolish if I dragged Kathleen all the way up to Cooney's house, and nobody appeared to eat my food?

Just for a time, that seemed to be what had happened.

We stood in the yard behind the house and shivered.

"She was inside," I said. "At least, that's where she came from."

"I'm not going in," said Kathleen. "Not after last time."

"I tell you it wasn't a ghost we heard breathing," I said. "It was Kate Cooney."

"Y-e-s," said Kathleen, not very enthusiastically.

"Anyway," I said, "I've come prepared, for I have my torch with me."

So I took out the torch, and after a bit more arguing,

74

talked Kathleen into coming through into the kitchen with me, that far at least.

"Then see how you feel," I said.

We went into the kitchen.

"Nobody here," said Kathleen.

"She must be around the house somewhere," I said.

"Well, you find her," Kathleen said. "I'm not," and she sat down on the chair.

"I can't very well go flashing my torch around the house," I said. "Samuel is getting the eggs now, and we have no right to be here at all. I heard Sean Brennan say he was going to keep an eye on things here, just in case the prowler reappeared . . . though I don't think any of our ones have much time for the prowler after what the wasps did to them."

"Call her name then," Kathleen said.

So I tried that.

No response.

"If this is one of your jokes," Kathleen said, in a threatening voice.

"It isn't, honestly it isn't."

"I'm going home," said Kathleen.

"Don't," I said. "She said she would . . ." then my voice trailed off, for the light of my torch had caught the dull glint of something on the table.

"Look!" I said.

Kathleen picked the bangle up.

"It's proof!" I said. "Look . . . there's a note!"

And there was too. It said "*For Kathleen, from Kate.*"

Chapter Seven

It was then, I suppose, that I made my biggest mistake.

I knew about the bangle. I knew it wasn't just a bangle, that there was something . . . *odd* . . . about it.

I should have told Kathleen about the thing that happened to me on Sleepers' Hill, the way the bangle seemed to take on a life of its own, and drag me across the field. I should have, but I was afraid of what she might say.

So I let her put the bangle on her arm, and walk home wearing it.

"Isn't it odd," said Kathleen, when we were down by the Ten Cottages again. She was holding her arm out straight, so that she could admire the bangle. "It feels all funny, somehow."

"I don't like it much," I said.

"I wonder where she got it."

"She said she found it," I said. "I think . . . I think you should take it off and keep it somewhere, Kathleen, just in case it wasn't Kate's to give."

"Don't be silly," said Kathleen. "I like it . . . only

there is something about it. It makes me feel . . . sort of all cold and shivery."

And she pulled the sleeve of her jersey down over the bangle, to cover it up.

That night I went to bed with my mind all in a muddle, and in the gap before I went to sleep I found myself worrying again about the bangle, and the Hill.

Maybe . . . maybe the bangle and the Hill were in some way connected?

Kate said she found it. What if she had found it there? But she wouldn't take anything from the Hill. No one would. No one from the Lanes would move so much as a stone from a place like that, priest or no priest, superstition or no superstition.

No one *from the Lanes* would . . . but Kate Cooney was a stranger. . . .

Chapter Eight

"You'll go up to Gilroy's Point Field this morning, Tom," said Big John the following morning. "Father Jennet will be sending up some papers for me, and you'll need to collect them off the bus."

"Indeed, and I will," I said.

"And listen now, Tom, you'll come straight back, and you will not be annoying the caravaners there, like your brother did."

"It was not Willie," I said. "For it was the four men from the caravans that made the trouble with Malachy Byrne and Dan Breen, and nothing to do with Willie at all."

"Willie is Willie," said my father. "He is a grown man now, and should have the sense to stay out of such things."

"Dan and Malachy would have called him coward," I said.

"Dan Breen has no more brain than one of his sows," my father said. "Dear help him, for he is not a bad man at heart, when he is off the bottle. But what is good enough for one of the Breens is not good enough for you and Willie, for I have tried what I could to show you what the likes of the Breens and the Coyles will not understand, that each man must live his own way, and let the man next to him do the same, without roaring and fighting at him."

"Margie Coyle says they have no right here at all, the caravaners," I said. "She said it was our fields they were on, and we should keep them off."

"You'll pay no heed to her, poor stupid woman," said Big John. "The caravaners are no better and no worse than anybody else, but they don't understand what they are at, because they are used to their towns and their offices and their factories. Half time when they do something wrong here, they don't know it, for it would not matter in the town, where there is neither crop nor cattle to protect, but just the concrete of the streets. It is a hard life they have in their factories, and indeed I don't know what your brother will make of it, if he goes."

"He will not go," I said. "I don't think so."

But my father shook his head, and in the end he was right.

I got Kathleen out from the back field, and we went up to the Point, past the cream and blue caravans sitting in their neat lines, with the washing strung out behind them. It is funny the way the city ladies cannot leave their washing behind them, but must wash away at it, even when they are supposed to be on holiday.

"You know my bangle," Kathleen said, bringing me back on to a subject I had no real desire to think about.

"I think it might be gold, and worth a lot of money."

"Och it is heavy, but just some cheap thing," I said.

"The thing in my mind," Kathleen said, "is that Kate may have more things like it up there, and if a burglar comes she would be a poor hand at stopping one."

I said nothing, for Kate Cooney had made a fair hand at stopping me with Joe Coyle's shot-gun . . . but then I'd taken the shot-gun back to Joe, if only to make sure that he didn't go searching for it at the house.

"If there are more things up there, we ought to tell Big John," Kathleen said. "It isn't fair. Somebody might hurt her if they break in, and she all alone."

"We don't even know that there is a treasure," I said. "And anyway I promised I wouldn't."

"I didn't though."

"I promised for you, Kathleen, you know I did."

"I don't think you can promise for someone," Kathleen said, tossing her hair.

"Well you can, because I did. Anyway it wouldn't be right. She gave you the bangle as a present. If she'd known you were going to give her away she wouldn't have been so nice about you."

"Was she nice about me?"

"She said your hair was nice," I said.

Kathleen thought about it a while.

"You're a vain thing," I said. "Just because she said your hair was nice you're prepared to say nothing about the bangle, and you'd have told otherwise."

"I wouldn't!"

"You mean you won't?"

"Well . . . not till we've asked her about it, anyway.

Maybe it is just an old bangle, and not worth anything."

When we got up to Gilroy's stores the bus was just pulling out, and Mr. Gilroy handed me a big brown packet marked with my father's name.

"From the Priest," he said.

We walked back along the Coastguard's Road, to have a look at the people in the caravans. There were some children there, but we took no notice of them. They were playing with a tennis racquet and a ball. Sea-siders are sea-siders, and you wouldn't know what they'd be up to next. If it isn't setting fire to the hay, it's leaving their rubbish stuffed in a ditch where the cows can get it and choke on the plastic bags . . . it is marvellous what a cow will try to eat if you give it the chance, and the worst thing of all is a plastic bag. You'd think some people had no homes of their own, the way they leave things around.

We met Pat Byrne the Insurance man coming down the road, and that was a surprise, for it wasn't his day. It turned out he left his car with the Breens, to have it fixed. The car was to be left back up that morning, but no sign of it appeared, so he'd come down from his house to the Ten Cottages, to see what was up.

As luck would have it, he found his car quicker than he thought he would, for as we turned off the Coastguard's Road to go down to the Cottages wasn't the car heading up at us, with Mickey Breen at the wheel, and the big fellow called Dick Spence, the one who'd clouted Willie, sitting in beside him.

"Stop! Stop!" cried Pat, bouncing out into the lane. But Mickey was in no mood for stopping, and shot right out into the road, forcing Pat to jump for his life, brief case and insurance book flying every which way. On went the car, and there was the one called Jimmy from the caravan camp grinning at us out of the back window, as Pat jumped about the road cursing and shaking his fist.

"What's happened?" said Kathleen, who had been lagging behind us.

"I tell you what's happened!" said Pat. "They're away off for a run in my motor, and me with the rounds to complete."

Kathleen gave a splutter of laughter before she could get her hand up to her mouth, and that only enraged him further. Truth to tell I was hard pressed not to burst out laughing myself, for Pat is a fat wee man and he was dancing about in the lane as if he might take off into the air any minute.

"It's only the sea-siders," I said.

"Oh and Breen! I saw him. Mickey Breen was at the wheel!" he spluttered. "Oh it's all right for Michael Breen riding round in his own customer's car, but how am I to do me work? Isn't there the weekly money to be picked up over half the country, and cows and hens and houses all going uninsured if I'm not round?"

"Will you come to the house and have a cup of tea, Pat?" said Kathleen, trying to make up for her giggles, but not really succeeding.

But he would not. He was off down the road fuming, with his cheeks puffed out and his black hair flopping around him, maybe hoping to pick up a sea-sider's lift on the way to Quinn's Bridge.

"You shouldn't have laughed at him like that, Kathleen," I said. "Pat's a decent man. Isn't our own cottage insured with him, not to speak of the burying money? Mickey Breen had no right going off in his car."

"That's funny company he's keeping, for a Breen," said Kathleen.

"He'll be charging them five bob a head, like a taxi," I said. Just the same it wasn't like the Breens to be mixing with a crowd like that, especially after the trouble with Malachy and Willie.

As we came down by the front of the Cottages mother was standing outside, looking for us.

"What kept you?" she said and then, as I went to explain about Pat, she shushed me. "Did you get the papers the Priest sent?"

"I did," I said.

"Well, hand them over then, for you're keeping the meeting waiting inside."

It was the first I had heard of any meeting, but when we went inside it was to find them all there, every man jack from the Cottages, from the biggest to the smallest, and Mrs. Weeney and Browbrook and the Hegans and all their kin, and quite a few of the mountain men as well . . . and every man with a look on him as if it was a funeral he was at.

My father took the packet from me, and bade me sit where I could. "You may hold your ground, children," he said. "For what has been said is a matter of as much importance to you as it is to anyone."

Then he walked over to the table, and opened out the

packet the Priest had sent him, spreading out some big white papers on the table top.

Peering over Dessie Owen's shoulder, I could make out that one of the papers was a big map, and it showed the mouth of the Lough, and the Point Field, and the Coastguard's Road . . . but it was all different.

My father started to speak.

"As you all well know," he said, "Father Jennet is a busy man, and not one to let the grass grow under his feet. Some like it, some don't. I have an open mind on it myself. You'll have heard tell of the sock factory there was to be, well, there is no sock factory, but now he's up to something else, and it may be that he'll bring it off."

There was a general murmur round the room, mostly of approval. Only Mrs. Weeney and Browbrook sat firm, and well they might, as Protestants.

"I take it," my father said, "that everyone here would be well pleased if he got the sock factory he was after, and fine jobs for everyone?"

Again there was a murmur of assent.

"We're all agreed then that something should be done," said my father, with a grave and unsmiling face. "The question that we've got to ask ourselves is what."

"Why?" said Joe Coyle. "I mean, what has it to do with us?"

"When all is said and done, Father Jennet is trying to help us, nobody else," said my father.

"He's all on for the people in Quinn's Bridge," muttered somebody.

"That's as maybe, he's priest here as well, now that

we have no one of our own, and we may look to him for leadership," said Big John, "if we're not fit to lead ourselves."

"I look to my own," said Mrs. Weeney, looking round her awkwardly, and truth to tell it must have been an odd position for the little soul. I wondered why my father had dragged down a Protestant to talk about priests.

"If we're not fit to lead ourselves," Big John repeated. "Now there's the rub. For the thing Father Jennet is proposing is one that affects every man here, and his wife and family. And if we don't have our say now, we never will, for it will be too late."

A silence fell on the room.

"Do you see this?" said my father, holding up a picture of a cottage with a straw roof, and a garage, and concrete patch around the front.

"This," he said, jabbing the picture with his finger, "this is what he's going to do to us!"

Nobody said anything.

"Central heating," my father said. "Car ports. Electric light, and cooking. A new road, and lavatories inside the house."

There was a stunned silence, for nobody quite understood what he was getting at.

Willie said, "It sounds fine to me."

Big John didn't seem to notice him.

"The only thing wrong with the scheme," he said, "is that we're all left out of it!"

There was a general gasp.

"How d'you mean, John Connor?" said Dessie.

And my father told him.

The scheme was simple enough. All the people were to be moved out of the Ten Cottages, and the houses along the Coastguard's Road. Every house was to be gutted, and a brand new shining inside put in, with hot water and light and central heating and garages . . . and our houses, our homes, were to be let out to the seasiders at twenty pounds a week.

Everybody wanted to speak suddenly, and nobody had anything very friendly to say about the Priest and his modern ideas, but it was my father who brought the conversation back to earth.

"There's very little we can do about it," he said. "It appears that it is to be a good thing for the whole area, for they will bring their money with them, and spend it in Quinn's Bridge, and the hotel and shops will do well. What is asked of us is a sacrifice, for the others here."

"It's more than that, Big John!" said Sean Brennan, his face gone red as a beetroot. "It is an outrage! These are our houses, and our land. They can't be sold out like that, to a pack of holiday-makers!"

My father looked grave. "What if it had been the sock factory?" he said.

"They would not have built the sock factory here!" said Sean Brennan.

"They would have built it somewhere," said my father. "Someone would have had to put up with it. It seems to me that we don't mind someone else having the bother, if we have the jobs."

"And what jobs do we get from holiday cottages?"

said Sean. "None at all, but all the bother is ours, and our homes gone into the bargain, for what man here can pay twenty pounds a week for his cottage?"

"You're right, Sean," said Joe Coyle, and it is not often this pair agree. "You should know better, Big John, than to say such a thing!"

"There would be jobs," said my father. "For the fields would still be here, and in the summer there would be parties to take out in the boats. Those who would stay would make fine money, and the rest . . . the rest would have gone already."

And he looked at Willie, who had not the face to stare him out, but lowered his gaze.

"You all know well that we are the rump of a people," said Big John. "Every year the young ones go, and they don't come back, for there is nothing here for them."

"You can't say that for the Breens!" said Joe. "We're still here."

"The thickest and the dumbest!" muttered Willie, but luckily Joe didn't hear him.

"It is true enough though," said Sean. "My own Eileen is in Northampton at the shoes, and young Fergus will go the same when he leaves the school."

"I know it well," said my father. "The question is should we go on as we are, and try to stop this plan, or should we give way and let the Priest do what he will, if it is to better the place for the others around us?"

"And where would we go?" demanded Margie Coyle, the first woman to speak, for our women do not have the way of interrupting in great talk.

87

"The Priest is to build us fine new houses at New Cross," Big John said. "For he has been to the Government, and they are to pay most. They will be fine houses, with stairs, and we will be close to Quinn's Bridge, and there will be money from the building when it happens, and a better place for the young ones when it is done."

"It is our lives too," said Margie Coyle. "We can't all be children, John Connor. I have lived in the Lanes all my life, and I have no wish to see things change."

That started them talking, and this one and that one all had to have their say . . . and were in the full flood of saying it, all talking at once, when who should walk in but Father Jennet himself, and with him who should it be but the man from Sloan's, with his black note book in his hand.

If I gave him a black look to match his book it was no more than he deserved, for now I understood the questions he had asked about the Lanes and the cottages, without the honest decency to tell me the reason for the asking.

"Well, John," said Father Jennet to my father, "and have you spread the news?"

"I have," said my father, "and it is not welcome, there is no gainsaying that."

"Priest or no priest," somebody muttered, and another said, "No priest."

"Perhaps I can explain," he said, "with the help of Professor McBride here, who is giving me a hand, so to speak." I'll say one thing for them, they talked with the golden tongue. The more they talked the more sensible it sounded, and the more we felt we ought to agree. Yet it seemed to me done in such a sleekit way, with McBride having me to take tea with him, and asking questions, that I found it hard to stomach. It was the loud-mouthed ones, the Joe Breens and the Dessies, who now found they had least to say. They were "No Father"ing and "Yes Father"ing around the room as though butter wouldn't melt in their gobs, eating out of Father Jennet's hand as he painted fine word pictures of the bright new houses we were to have in Quinn's Bridge. Then it was your man McBride, with a little box of slides, showing us what the cottages would be like, when he had them fitted out and changed entirely. That was a bad business altogether. My father said very little, for I think he thought of himself as the spokesman for the Priest, as he had been appointed to explain to the others before Father Jennet came himself. It was a wise enough move on the Priest's part, I know, but I felt my father had a bitterness in it. The one to take up the challenge was my brother Willie.

"Tell me, Father," he said. "Is it done yet, or still no more than these bits of paper?"

"The contracts remain to be signed, William Connor," said Father Jennet. "But I have no doubt they will be."

"And if we will not leave the Ten Cottages?"

"You are leaving yourself, Willie," said the Priest. "The say is not yours. The say is with these people . . . no, that is not true, entirely. The say is with me, and the owner of the land, and these people to decide what would be the best for all."

"You cannot do it!" Willie objected.

My father raised his head, and frowned. "Though it saddens me to say it, I think we must. For it would be a good thing."

"Aye," said Joe Brown. "Somewhere else it would, but not here!"

"We cannot pass our ill luck on to others, Joe," said my father. "I do not want it, but I will not raise a finger to stop it, for things must grow."

There was a silence.

"I will!" I said suddenly, for I felt all hot and rushed about it. "I'll not let you do it!"

"Hold your wheest!" said my mother sharply.

"Let him have his say," said the Priest, with a smile.

I was half afraid about what I'd done, but there was nothing for it but to go straight on, now I'd started.

"I don't want to see holiday people in our houses," I said. "I agree with Willie. It should not be. I'll . . . I'll do something about it, so I will."

"Tom!" said my mother, in disapproval.

"I want to live here," I said.

Willie remained silent.

Half a dozen people started talking all at once. I was fed up with them and their talk. I ran out the door and into the Harp Field, and it was there my father found me an hour later, when all the rest had gone away.

"I won't let them," I said.

"Perhaps you are right," he said. "If I was your age I might feel the same. You may do what you can, young Tom. I won't spite you. But I doubt you will stop it, for the Father has the town behind him, and the extra business is wanted in Quinn's Bridge."

"He cannot do it to our homes."

"He can."

"I won't let it. I'll . . . I'll go to the man that owns the land, and tell him not to sell."

"Then you will be a bright boy," my father said. "For the owner is not to be found, and till he is there will be no building here."

"I hope he may stay unfound," I said.

"That may be, Tom," my father said. "It well may be. For Cooney's had the land, and sold it off, and the one bright thing in it all is that the man who bought it cannot be found."

"What was his name?" I said.

"Hervey," said my father. "Some man from the South. Hervey was his name."

"I shall find Hervey," I said.

"You may walk a long way," said my father, dryly.

Chapter Nine

If the Lord in his Heaven was a reasonable man at all you would think he would have seen that the news of Father Jennet's plan was enough disaster for one day, but indeed he did not!

There was more to come, and it came in the shape of Mrs. Weeney's Samuel and Mrs. Weeney, all done up in their hats and coats, parading down the lane to our house, just when we were sitting down to our tea.

They called Big John to the door, and when Big John came back in it was with a small sullen face beside him.

Kate!

The way he told it, Samuel had found her in the garden, and had a struggle with her when she tried to get away. He brought her to my father as all the people in the Lanes did, thinking he would know what to do with her.

"She may stay here," said my father.

But Kate didn't look pleased.

She would speak to no one, but I could see from her glance and the way she curled up her lip that I was held to blame for her being caught out!

Chapter Ten

So it was that Kate came to be in our house, which was small enough to begin with, and hardly had room for another one . . . though mind you the Breens managed well enough in a house the same size, and there were eight of them.

It meant that Kathleen had to share the bed in the end room with her, but Kathleen didn't seem to mind . . . in fact she was delighted, for Kate was somebody to talk to.

Kate talked to her too, a bit anyway, which was more than she would to anyone else. Whatever I might say she would have it that I had sent Samuel Weeney up to catch her. But even with Kathleen, Kate had not much to say, but must needs bide her tongue.

"You're not to pester the child, do you hear," Big John said, when he had us alone one day. "She's a funny quiet creature, and there will maybe be big changes coming in her life, for I doubt the aunt will not be able to look after her any more, and she must find a new place to lay her head."

"Couldn't she stay here?" Kathleen asked.

My father shook his head. "There would be her own parents to consider," he said. "Wherever they may be. Miss Cooney will have to tell us that, for the child either does not know, or will not say a word. But there will be someone to look after her, I have no doubt."

As far as everything else went, all was quiet. There was no more news about the plans, although the word came through that a town lawyer was searching out the owner of the land. I wished bad cess on him, and left it at that, for there seemed to be nothing I could do. Somehow I couldn't bring myself to believe it would ever happen.

But I wasn't happy in myself, and neither was Kathleen. I doubt if either of us could have put a name on it, but I had my own ideas. Somehow the old bangle was always there at the back of my mind and, although Kathleen would say nothing much, I had the feeling it was the same with her. One night, about half-past two, I caught her up by the window, rubbing her arm.

"What is it you are at, Kathleen?" I whispered.

"It is the ould bangle," she said. "For it will not let me sleep, and is nipping at my arm."

"I'll get someone," I said, sitting up, but she shushed me down, and would hear no more, in case it might wake Kate.

I asked her about it in the morning, but she said I'd been dreaming, that it was all nonsense, and that she would NOT give the bangle back to Kate, and tell her to return it where it came from.

"It probably came from a shop," she said. "Kate would look silly trying to sell it back."

"I don't think it did," I said, and later I asked Kate straight out where it had come from, but she would say nothing about it, except that I was fussing about nothing, and it was a strange way to repay generosity, for it was her present to Kathleen.

"You told me you found it," I said. "But you didn't say where."

"It is none of your business," she said.

"I think I know where you found it," I said. "And if I am right, I think you should take it back, for it is not lucky to take things from a place like that, that is not an ordinary place."

"You are just a nuisance, Tom, and indeed I will not," she said, and off she went.

The more I thought about it, the surer I was that the bangle would have to go back. The only pity is that I didn't do something about it, there and then.

But truth to tell my mind was not on bangles, for the big excitement of the match in Aghbo was almost on us. There was the question of how we were to go to it and, of course, how Willie would play against the very best boys in the county. He said very little about it himself, but the men at the crossroads could speak of no other. Mick, Joe, Dan and all the Breens were going, as were Joe Coyle and Dessie and the Brennans, and Mrs. Weeney's Samuel came across the fields to wish Willie good luck, even though he couldn't go himself, being of the other sort. At first Peter Watson would have it that we should hire a bus from the bus company, but then it seemed that this would cost too much, and it was decided that the Breens would get three motor-cars from Maxie Hartnett's garage in Quinn's Bridge, and all from the Ten Cottages who wished to go would travel in them, each passenger to pay thirty pence a head for the petrol . . . though no doubt the Breens would find some way to make a profit on it.

Willie, of course, would travel with the team in Father Jennet's bus, and my father and I were to go with Mickey Breen, but there remained the problem of Kate.

"I'd rather the child wasn't taken to a strange place at all," said my mother. "For she has had enough upset for one lifetime."

I knew what she meant, for Kate was still timid as a mouse, and apt to go off into corners and keep her own counsel. She seemed scared by the sea-siders fooling round the beach, and would say scarce a word to anyone at Ten Cottages but Kathleen, even though she might have seen that we were doing our best to be friendly.

It was Kathleen herself who settled the matter, for she declared that she would stay at home with Kate, for she was not minded to go to the match. I thought it was a miserable thing that Willie's own sister should not see his hour of glory, but just the same it seemed to be the wisest thing to do. So it was arranged; Kathleen would stay, and the rest of us would go.

"I think it very good of you, Kathleen," I said to her as we walked up the lane towards Mrs. Weeney's Post Office, where I was to draw fifty pence from my savings for the big day out.

"I'll have the cottage to myself," said Kathleen. "Won't that be something! And Kate and I will have a chance to talk to each other."

"She doesn't talk."

"She talks to me."

"I bet she doesn't really."

"Well, not much," Kathleen admitted, "but now and then. She was telling me how she used to go to a big school, before she came to Miss Cooney. I don't think she's been long at Cooney's, though she doesn't seem too sure. She says Miss Cooney wouldn't let her out of the house, much. They played cards, and she helped with the hens, and Miss Cooney gave her lessons."

"Did she say anything about her parents?"

"No," Kathleen shook her head, "but she sort of hinted. I think they're both dead. She said something about a lawyer putting her on a bus. I think she was left to Miss Cooney, only nobody knew about it."

"I don't think you can leave people to people," I said.

"Yes you can," said Kathleen. "Legal Guardians, that's what it is called. If anything were to happen to Big John and Mother, we'd be left to the Connors up the Hill, so we would."

I don't like the Connors up the Hill, and I said so.

"Anyway," Kathleen said, "that's not the point. The point is what will happen to Kate."

"They might let her stay with us."

"You heard what Father said," Kathleen said. "They mightn't let her stay with us, if she is an orphan. Our house would not be grand enough, maybe. The Welfare would not let us have her."

"Our house is grand enough," I said.

"They wrote about our houses in the paper, and said they were no good because there were no drains."

"Our house is better than Miss Cooney's."

"Miss Cooney was left Kate, that's the difference," Kathleen said. "She would have to be given to us, and they won't do that. She'll have to go to an orphan home if Miss Cooney stays in hospital."

"But she isn't an orphan, not if she's got some family. And Miss Cooney is her family. Proper orphans have nobody but themselves, and she has Miss Cooney, and it doesn't matter a bit if Miss Cooney is mad. I expect that is why Kate is so keen on Miss Cooney, because Miss Cooney stops her from being an orphan."

We came up to Mrs. Weeney's Post Office, and there was Professor McBride's tricycle parked outside. Well, I had a mind not to go in at all, seeing it there, but on the other hand I wasn't going to be put off my rightful way by any man, even if he was two-faced and scheming to take our houses away from us.

So in we went.

He was standing by the counter, doing up a big brown parcel, no doubt with the undoing of our houses in it.

"Ah," he said. "Good morning, John Connor's Tom!"

I sniffed and stuck my head in the air, to show I was having none of that.

"He's not talking to you," said Kathleen. "For you are taking away our houses, and neither of us will be having anything to do with you."

He looked startled, and well he might.

"That's quite right," I said. "You had no business asking me questions like that, when all you meant was to take our land and our place away."

Then I turned back to Mrs. Weeney, and handed her my Savings Book, just as calm and polite as you please.

"You mustn't take it that way," he said.

"We will take it as we please," I said.

"And so will others," said Mrs. Weeney, looking at him over her glasses. It was plain to see he had no welcome there, though doubtless she would have fine business from the holiday-makers, if ever they came to have our houses.

"There you are now," said Kathleen.

He put down his parcel without a word, and went out.

When we came out of Weeney's he was standing by his tricycle, as if he was waiting for us.

"John Connor's Tom," he called.

"I have no mind to talk with you, Professor," I said. "For professor or not, you are not an honest man."

He flushed at that, and I think I caught him to the quick with it. We walked down the road, and he walked after us.

As we came by McArt's Bridge Kathleen nudged me, and said, "We cannot keep on, Tom, for it is no way to treat a gentleman, and a professor from the town."

"Indeed I can," I said.

"Well, I cannot," she said, and turned back to him.

By the time we reached the Cottages I was the odd man out, for they were chatting like old friends, and she ran to our house as we came by, and bade him wait his time.

I passed on down on to the beach and stood there moodily, looking at the waves, for I felt it was nothing but a betrayal.

Then she was out of the house again, and showing him something . . . and I could see it was Kate's bangle. A thing we would have done better to keep to ourselves, in my opinion.

Well, I was determined that there would be none of that, so I went back to them.

"Well," he said, examining the bangle, "John Connor's Tom, what have we here?"

I could have told him, right enough, the whole story . . . but I doubt if he would have believed me. "It is my bangle as much as hers," I said. "And I would like you to hand it to me, if you please." Very stiff I was, to show him I was demanding, not asking.

"He says it is a rare thing, Tom, and very old."

"Indeed it is none of his business."

"You are right of course, Tom," he said. "It is nothing to do with me. But it would interest some people I know, for it is very old, and belongs in a museum. It is much much older than you might think, and these markings . . . well. . . ."

"Well, you cannot have it," I said. "It is not ours to give." Then I grabbed the bangle from him, and like a shot I was away, with Kathleen after me. He shouted out, but he did not try to follow us.

"Why did you do that, Tom?" she said. "It is indeed our bangle, for Kate gave it to me, and I will give it away if I like."

"You will not," I said. Then, as we walked along the

beach, I told her all I knew about the bangle, and what had happened to me, and what I thought.

"I think it is bad thing, an unfortunate thing, and it should not have been taken from the Hill," I said. "It is like the fairy thorn tree Bridie Whelan moved, and the next day her bullock got on the road in front of Davie's van and bust all his eggs and a fortnight later the goat died, and Paddy Whelan got the measles and was spots for weeks. It is like that. It is a thing no man should move, for it belongs where it belongs."

"I don't think I believe in that sort of thing," said Kathleen, being grown up.

"You've talked enough about it nipping at you," I said. "And you know fine well what the Hill is like. Kate got it from there, and Kate must get it back!"

We sat down on the sandbank against the Point Field wall.

"If it is old, it must be worth a lot of money," Kathleen said, ruefully. "And we are to give it away, just like that."

"Your professor would not say how valuable it was," I said. "But you may count on it that if a man from the city university is after it, it must be worth something, for it is not for nothing they have their fancy cars and black fishy stuff that costs pounds more than it is worth."

"If it is a precious thing . . ." Kathleen said.

"It is a misfortunate thing."

"Maybe Kate didn't get it from the Hill," she said.

"Well, we'll see about it," I said, and I stood up . . . or maybe something made me stand up, I don't know, for it was to find myself face to face with Dick Spence from the caravans, who must have heard every word we had been saying.

"You were listening to us!" I said, as he came forward.

"That's a nice thing you have there," he said, stepping toward me.

"Run, Tom," said Kathleen, and wasn't she right? I did not stand on the order of my going, but took to my heels for the second time that day, for fear he would have the bangle off me to sell to someone in the city.

The sea-sider was easy enough to outspeed, and we arrived back at Ten Cottages to find Kate sitting by the window, with her face as long as the winter.

"I wanted to speak to you about the bangle, Kate," I began, but Kathleen stopped me.

"Can't you see something is wrong?" she said. "What is it, Kate? What is the matter?"

"None of your business," said Her Majesty, snappily enough.

"Oh well, I will not let it fuss me then," I said, but the next minute she was crying, and I was sorry I had been so curt. I did not know where to put myself, but Kathleen took her over to the sofa, and shooed me away.

I went out to the back, where Willie was cleaning his boots.

"What is the matter with Kate?" I said.

"Father Jennet came. He says that they will not let Miss Cooney away, and she must stay in the hospital for now."

"Oh," I said.

Then I went back in.

"I am sorry for your trouble, Kate," I said, holding out my hand, as polite as could be.

"Go away, Tom," said Kathleen, and I don't know what it was about me, but the words I'd said were hardly out before Kate started crying again as though her heart would burst there and then. But then I suppose I do know.

There was no time for anything more, for within the half-hour the cars were at the door, with a different Breen at each wheel, and we were off for the match.

There is a long story . . . the match! Here is not the time to tell it, and wasn't it all in the newspapers anyway? Truth to tell it was not the triumph it might have been, for Willie had a kick in the side before he was ten minutes on, and that shook the wind out of him. He had a fine point in the second half, but was never at his best, and it was a subdued John Connor's Tom who rode back in the car.

I suppose I had been expecting too much of the match. In my mind I had Willie at Croke Park in the All-Ireland final, with me in the seat of honour in the stand, beside the President, and calling out for our county. Truth to tell, it did not work out as badly as I thought, for after the game the name of Connor was on the team sheet, though not to play. Willie was to travel to Clones with the team, and be reserve if any should fall out. It was fine, but it was not the cloud of glory I had cast for him, and seemed a poor thing.

However, if it was, you may pardon me for skipping

it, for truth to tell the big story of the day was at Ten Cottages.

When we got home, it was to find the front door wide open and Kathleen standing at it, talking to the Sergeant from Quinn's Bridge. A police car was drawn up at the side of the lane, and two more policemen were walking across the Harp Field.

"Oh John, John!" cried my mother.

My father was out of the car before it stopped, and over to Kathleen.

"What is it, child?" he asked. "What's the matter?"

The matter was that Kate was gone, run away . . . and behind her she had left a house that looked as if a hurricane had hit it. Every drawer in the place had been emptied out, and the very pillows on the beds had been ripped open.

"What for?" I said. "I don't understand!"

"I don't know," said Kathleen sadly. She was pale, and tense. She bit her lip, then she burst out. "It is the bangle, Tom. Nothing is right since we got the bangle! Every last thing keeps going wrong!"

Chapter Eleven

We sat around the range, Willie picking the mud off his football boots, Kathleen brushing her hair, and myself whittling away at a piece of wood.

It was half-past eight, and we were under orders to stay in, in case Kate should come back.

"What will happen to her?" Kathleen asked.

"It is a poor thing to do," I said. "Imagine tearing up our house, and running away like that, when we were being kindly to her."

Willie said nothing, but scraped away, letting the mud from his boots fall on to an old bit of newspaper.

We were all sad about it, and at a loss to know what had come over her, for by Kathleen's word she was sitting on the chair reading most of the afternoon, and seemed no different when Kathleen went to Weeney's for the paraffin . . . only to come back and find that Kate had left us, all in a rush, and throwing all our furniture round the cottage after her.

In she went to the professor, not knowing what to do, and he it was who went to Gilroy's and rang through to

Quinn's Bridge, though I think my father felt at first that it should not have been done.

That would have been all well, if Kate had been found. But the plain fact was that she had disappeared about five o'clock, and she was still not to be found.

"I suppose they've searched the house?" I said.

"Don't be silly," said Willie. "Of course they have. Wouldn't it be the first place anyone would look?"

"She hid there before," I said. "The men couldn't find her."

"That's true," said Willie.

"I wish they would let me try," said Kathleen. "She talks to me."

"She didn't tell you she was going to throw all our furniture round the house!" I said, impatiently. I was sorry for Kate Cooney, but you can have too much of a good thing.

"Just the same," Kathleen said.

"Just the same what?"

"If she was hiding, she would come out for me," Kathleen said. "And you said yourself, she's good enough at hiding for them not to find her."

"The Sergeant would find her," Willie said.

"He would not," said Kathleen.

I poked the range grate, and looked at the red flames flickering. It was warm and cosy inside, and terrible to think of Kate wandering around out in the cold.

"What made her run away?" said Willie.

"Her aunt, and everything," said Kathleen. "She was upset about going into a home."

"She could have stayed with us," I said.

"She could not," said Willie. "For Big John asked about it, and the Priest says that if she is not with Miss Cooney who is her own flesh, she must be with the Welfare, and they would not let her come here, for they do not like our old houses."

"There is nothing wrong with our houses," I said, furious with them for their fussiness. Our little houses are as nice as theirs in the city.

"The Priest will knock them down anyway," said Willie.

"If they're so fussed about drains, why not give us some?" I grumbled.

"They like knocking old things down," said Kathleen, stirring the fire.

We sat silent for a minute.

"We ought to do something about Kate," I said, breaking the silence.

"We ought to find her," Kathleen said. "That is the most important thing. I don't like to think of Kate being out in the night like that, maybe scared and frightened."

"She should not have run away," said Willie.

"Maybe she didn't," Kathleen said. "Maybe she was kidnapped or something."

"And for why would she be kidnapped?" he said. "You'll be telling me next Kate Cooney has a terrible secret."

I looked at Kathleen, and Kathleen looked at me. Her hand went to her sleeve, where I could make out the bulge of the old metal bangle. Kate had a secret . . . but who could want to know about it?

The professor.

"I'm for a bit of air," I said, and went out. Kathleen was quickly after me. She caught my arm. "It isn't him!" she said. "He's gone home."

"Who else then?"

"I don't know. But that must be it!"

"We'll have to find her ourselves," I said. "She's much more likely to come out if we're looking for her than anyone else. She doesn't trust anyone else."

*   *   *

It was cold as we came over the fields, for there was a wind blowing, and the night was already dark around us. Our feet sank in the furrows, and we passed little enough talk between us.

"There will be someone at the house, you know," I said. "I heard Big John say that one of the men would keep watch there, in case she came back."

"It is still the best place to start," said Kathleen.

"She likely has a hidey hole up there somewhere," I said. "Perhaps if she sees us, she'll come out."

We came over the wall of Cooney's field, and started round the edge as usual. The tree on Sleepers' Hill stuck out against the night sky, and gave me just the tail end of a shiver.

I was about to say something to Kathleen about it, when she turned to me.

"I don't like it here," she said.

"What do you mean? Because of the Hill?"

"Maybe it is the rotten old bangle," she said. "It is tight and cold around my arm and . . . and . . . I don't know. It is as if it was alive sometimes, you see, for there's a throb gets in it."

"Maybe it is your blood stopped from going round," I said.

"Take a hold of my arm, Tom," she said. "For I feel funny, all of a sudden."

So I took a tight grip on her arm, and marched around the side of the field. Half time she had her eyes closed, and her teeth gripped tight, and I knew well what she was feeling, for hadn't I been through it myself?

"There's no doubt about it," I said. "Kate must put it back where it came from, or we'll have no peace. She who took it must return it, for that is what the old tales say."

"Where is she, though?" Kathleen muttered.

We got to the wall with no incident, bar the sudden rush of a hare, which startled me half out of my skin, for it leapt from almost under my feet.

"I wonder if one of the men is at the house?" I said. "I had a notion back there that I saw a flash of light at the window."

"I didn't," said Kathleen, which wasn't surprising, for she had had her eyes shut most of the time. She had her hand clasped tight round the bangle on her arm.

"Why are we whispering?"

"Because we are," she whispered back.

We came out at the side of the house, the gravel crunching under our feet.

"Quiet," I said. "We may creep up on her!"

Round the side of the house we crept.

The kitchen door was open and . . . and there was

somebody sitting in the chair, by the table . . . but it didn't look like Kate!

"Stop!" I hissed.

We stood where we were.

"Who is it?" Kathleen asked.

"I don't know . . . a man."

"Maybe it is one of the policemen," said Kathleen.

"I don't think a policeman would be just sitting there."

We crept a little closer. There was something funny about the way the man sat there. He was slumped forward, his chin on his chest.

"Stay here, Kathleen," I said.

"I'm as brave as you are," she protested.

I stepped up to the door, and coughed, loudly.

The man did not stir.

"Hullo," I said.

Not a movement.

"Maybe he's ill," Kathleen said. "Or asleep."

But he wasn't ill, or asleep. He was tied to the chair, with a camping rope. I could see it now, wound several times round his body. And the reason he did not reply to us was that he was unconscious, with a sack over his head!

"Quick," I said, and we darted in to him. It was the work of a moment to get the sack off his head.

"Sean!" I exclaimed. "Sean Brennan!"

But Sean did not stir.

"Get the ropes off him, quick, Kathleen," I said.

But she had frozen to the spot, and did not move.

"Listen!"

Someone was coming.

"Quick!" I said, and pulled open the door . . . there was nothing else for it. Somebody had knocked Sean Brennan out and tied him up, we couldn't let that someone catch us.

We went through the door into the dark at the foot of the stone steps, and then up them into the hall where we had stood before.

"Out the other way," said Kathleen. "The way we came in before."

"Who is that?" said a voice in the dark, and a light appeared down the hall, between us and the door. It was someone carrying a caravan oil lamp, one of the little ones with the handle at the side. The flame flickered in the breeze through the open door.

"It's me," said a voice behind us, from the kitchen. "What kept you?"

"I was looking for the girl. She got away from us."

The man in the hall cursed.

I heard the kitchen door open, and someone start up the steps we had just come up . . . it was the one called Jimmy, from the caravans.

The one with the oil lamp came slowly down the hall toward us.

Jimmy came up the stone steps, feeling his way in the dark.

We were caught in the middle!

There was only one thing for it . . . the stairs. I think we both thought of it at the same moment. There was nowhere else to go.

"Up!" I hissed.

"What's that?" said Jimmy.

"What?" said the other one, and the lamplight flashed down the long hall as he raised it.

We pressed back against the wall.

"I think the girl is here," said Jimmy. "I think I heard her."

I pulled Kathleen by the hand, and we got up three or four stairs.

"There!" shouted Jimmy.

The lamplight caught us in the full glare.

"Those kids!" said the man with the lamp, and in that moment I saw his face. It was Dick Spence from the caravans, who had listened in to our conversation.

"Stay where you are!" he said.

"Well, well," said Dick. "If the girl wouldn't tell us where the pretty things are kept, perhaps these two will."

"Up, Kathleen," I said and started up the stairs.

"After them!" cried Dick . . . and after us they came, crashing up the stairs.

There was a long corridor at the top, with dark doors opening off it. We blundered along it, and were half-way down when the other two appeared at the top of the stairs.

"There they go!" cried Jimmy.

"Split up!" I ordered Kathleen.

I went through one door, she went on down the corridor.

"Get him," cried the one called Dick.

I slammed the door behind me, and looked to see if there was any way out. There was . . . but it was no use.

Wasn't it like the thing that the room I chose to escape into should be one with bars on the window?

"Ouch!" I heard Kathleen shout.

The door swung open, and I could see Dick framed in it.

"Come on, kid," he said. "We've got you both now."

"Indeed you have not," I said, and leapt at him, pummelling as best I could.

I caught him a kick on the leg that made him yowl and stagger back, but as he went he grabbed at me, and I fell on top of him.

"Lay off!" he cried. "I'll crack you one!"

I hit him as hard as I could, and wriggled free. I was half-way to my feet and making for the stairs, when I saw two more of them were standing there, laughing at me.

"Little kid knocked you down, Dickie!" said one.

I stood where I was, panting.

"Take that for your trouble," said Dick, and he caught me a terrific buffet round the ear, that knocked me sideways on to the ground and set my head reeling.

"Bring them down to the big room," he ordered the other two.

I was half dragged, half carried between them down the corridor to the big room at the end, where Kathleen was already with Jimmy, who had put the oil lamp on top of an old packing case.

"Well, well," he said. "Two out of the three! And where is the other one?"

"I don't know," I said. "And if I did know I wouldn't tell, so there!"

"Listen, cock," he said. "You'd better button your lip, if you don't want trouble."

"Jimmy," said Dick, standing by the door. "Here a minute. I want a word. I have an idea that'll fix them."

Jimmy frowned at him. "There's only one idea we need," he said. "We need these kids to tell us where they get their fancy ornaments from."

"Just the same," said Dick. "Come out here a minute."

Jimmy shrugged, and went out to join the other three in the corridor, closing the door behind him . . . but not before he'd picked up the lamp. We were left in darkness.

"I don't understand," Kathleen said.

"I do!" I said. "Dick Spence heard us talking about the bangle, didn't he? He must have decided that there was more stuff hidden somewhere, the only question was where. So he waited around until we'd gone to the match, and then they paid a visit to our house and turned it upside down looking. They didn't find anything except Kate, and they must have put two and two together and come here with her . . . only she managed to get away from them. Still, they thought they were in the right place, so they knocked Sean out and tied him up, and started searching. And we walked in in the middle."

"How do we get out?" Kathleen said.

"We don't," I said.

"There must be a window," Kathleen said.

Well, there was, but it looked high for jumping out of. Looking down, we could see the roof of the kitchen and the yard. I wondered if Sean had come round yet. Probably not. There had been a funny smell about him, as though they'd drugged him, or done some such thing. I don't know much about that, but I've seen it on Samuel's television set.

The window above the kitchen . . . there was something. . . .

The door opened again, and the four men came in.

"Well, kids," said Dick, "we've had our chat and we reckon you'll have to stay here, alone, for a night or two, just to think it over. We don't want to hurt you, and you won't come to any harm here alone, at night, with rats and mice and what not, will you? On the other hand, if you give us the word, we'll let you go straight home."

"Oh yes?" I said, looking round me. Where was it? It had to be somewhere high up. The lamplight moved, as he put it back on the packing case.

"I hope you're going to be helpful," said Jimmy. "Because if you aren't. . . ."

There it was . . . just over the window, a grey shadowy bump against the woodwork.

"You can start by giving us the bangle."

"I will not," Kathleen said.

"Don't be silly, Kathleen," I said.

"I . . ."

"Give it me," I said.

"I will not."

"You will," I said.

"That's a sensible boy," said Jimmy.

"Come on, Kathleen," I said. "Hand over."

Kathleen pulled the bangle off her arm, and reached out with it toward Jimmy . . . but I was too quick for her, and grabbed it.

"Hey!" said Dick.

I knew I had only the one chance, and could only hope I'd make it. I've always been a fair hand with a stone, but I never thought it would come to matter so much.

I threw the bangle over-arm, straight and hard . . . right into the wasps' nest!

"You mad kid!" said Jimmy, stepping forward. "What do you. . . ."

But he found out, all too quickly.

There was an angry buzzing sound, and then they were on us, what seemed like thousands and thousands of angry wasps, disturbed for the second time in a week, and out for revenge.

"Ahh!" screamed Jimmy, as the first half-dozen lit on him all in a bunch.

Dick struck out blindly, staggered backwards and fell over the packing case, knocking down the lamp.

I grabbed Kathleen, and thrust her toward the window. High up or not, it would have to do.

"No," she said.

"But yes!" I said.

The next minute we were up on the sill, and off it, falling down into the darkness to land on the kitchen roof. "Ooooh, my ankle!" said Kathleen.

"Lie there," I said.

The kitchen door banged, and we saw the first two of them go out through it, running like mad and plunging through the grass toward the fields. Dick came next, furiously beating round his head, and last was Jimmy, running and panting and falling over himself.

When they had gone, we dropped down into the yard.

"Do you think they'll come back?" Kathleen said, feeling her ankle.

"I do not," I said.

Then we heard it . . . a crackling sound, that quickly turned to a roar.

"What. . . ?"

"Look, Tom!" Kathleen cried, pointing up at the room we had jumped out of.

Red flames licked the window, and black smoke poured out. The house was old and eaten dry with worm, and the falling lamp must have lit it like dry tinder. Smoke and flame belched out.

There was only one thing to do, and that was obvious. We had to get help.

At least that was what seemed obvious to us. We ran as fast as we could round the side of the house, and were half-way down the lane to Weeney's when I realized the mistake we had made.

"Stop!" I said. "Kathleen, stop. We've got to go back!"

"Go back? What do you mean?"

"Sean . . . Sean Brennan . . . he's inside! He'll burn to death!"

"Oh Tom . . ."

"You go on!" I ordered. "You get help. I'm going back for him. Don't argue . . . go!"

And she went.

I doubt if I have ever covered ground faster than I did on my way back to Miss Cooney's house, but as I came in sight of it, I feared I was too late. The blaze was bright now, and must have spread through the old and rotting timbers like wildfire. There was a stiff breeze fanning the flames, and the heat of it hit me in a great wave.

Sean . . . would he be dead already, and he tied to the chair, and not able to move a limb?

There was nothing for it but to go straight on in and get him out.

I rounded the side of the house, ran down, and turned round the back. Flame licked out through the open kitchen door, and as I stood there the window cracked in the heat, with a sound like Joe Coyle's shot-gun.

I ripped off my coat and wound it round my arm. Then I took a deep breath and dived in.

The heat was terrible. The smoke got up my nose and into my chest, and my inside felt like an oven. I could feel my skin prickle. Something fell against my ear. Then I was in the middle of the room, and bumping into Sean.

He was on the ground, with the chair still tied to him, and he moaned and clutched at me.

I grabbed at him, and hauled. He moved a bit, then the chair stuck. I pulled again . . . it would hardly move. It came free suddenly, and I stumbled and lost my footing. My jersey was burning. Smoke got into my mouth, and made me cough and choke, and I got on to my knees, still tugging at Sean, and I could feel the heat off the floor like a griddle and. . . .

Somebody caught at me . . . and hauled. It was Kate Cooney, her black hair plastered round her face, pulling for all she was worth and pulling . . . and pulling.

I remember the air hitting me, and eating down inside my chest, and somebody rolling me over and over on the ground to put the fire out on my clothes, and Dan Breen standing in the light of the flames with half his hair burned off, and Kate cradled in his arms like a baby.

There was Sean, held between Joe Coyle and Willie, looking all in, and Big John bending over me, and talking in my ear.

The last thing I heard was the clang of the fire engine, come all the way over from Darkwater.

Chapter Twelve

There we were, myself and Kate Cooney, installed in the two single beds in the big room, with a roaring fire . . . and all set as the heroes of the hour!

It was the best sort of being a hero, for neither of us had come to any great harm. I had a burn on my neck that I could have done without, and Kate was badly shaken . . . though she talked more that morning than I had ever heard her talk before.

And hadn't we plenty to talk about!

Kathleen was in by us, seeing us well settled, and treating us like bone china, when my father came through the door.

"I've a visitor for Kate!" he said.

Well, it is a queer thing, and one I have no understanding of, but when Kate saw Miss Cooney coming through the door, half propped up with a crutch, her face lit up like the sun and the moon and the stars, all washed together and hung on a line! And if there was one as well pleased as Kate, it was the old woman, who shushed off all polite inquiries from my mother with a wave of her crutch.

"Didn't I walk out on them!" she said. "I'm not staying in their hospital, and my niece in flames! 'Lie down,' said they, 'I will not,' said I! And I upped and away like the wind to see my Kate, and here I am!"

"You may sit down and rest yourself, Miss Cooney," said my father anxiously, "and not fret yourself!"

"I'll do that, John Connor," she said, and sat herself back in my father's kitchen chair with a little gasp of relief, for truth to tell she looked hard pressed enough, for all her talk of outwitting the doctors.

"They'll be out after me in their ambulance, John Connor," she said. "But you may tell them from me, I'm not moving."

My father looked at my mother, and my mother didn't know where to look.

"You know the house is gone, Miss Cooney?" he said. "It's to the ground, you'll not live there again."

"Oh aye," she said, "I know that. But there's more than one house in the world. I see round me in the row two fine cottages, John Connor, and I know no reason why I shouldn't stop in them, if you're not grown too grand in Ten Cottages to have the likes of a Cooney."

"It isn't as simple as that," my father said.

"Oh but it is," cackled Miss Cooney. "The old house is gone well enough, but Pat Byrne knows I have my payments in the book. Oh, I'm not as mad as I look! There's a pretty penny to come there, far and away more than I need to buy the cottage."

"Wouldn't that be great?" said Kathleen, all smiles. "You'll live here next door, Kate, and between the lot of us we'll look after your aunt."

"You will not," said Miss Cooney stoutly. "Haven't I always looked after myself?"

"The doctors . . ." said Kathleen.

"Fiddle-de-dee to the doctors!"

"You mean you'd buy Sloan's Cottage, and live there?" said my father slowly. "Move in down here?"

"And why not? The house is insured, and the house is burned down. Isn't that what it was insured for?"

"Aye," said my father.

"What's wrong?" said Miss Cooney. "Is there any reason for why I should not?"

My father stood up. "There is," he said. "For you may as well know now, Miss Cooney, that the man Hervey that bought the land from your father is to sell out to Father Jennet, and soon the Cottages will be no use to any of us, but only for the visitors."

"They will not," said Miss Cooney firmly.

"Oh but they will," said my father. "Hasn't he the contracts drawn up, and ready to be signed?"

"Mr. Hervey will sign nothing," she said. "For Mr. Hervey is dead and gone, poor man. . . ."

"Are you sure?"

"Wasn't he my brother-in-law?" she snapped, banging with her stick, and then pointing it at Kate. "Isn't that his own child there, left on my hands?"

"But . . . but. . . ."

"Every bit of ground around here belongs to her, John Connor," she said. "And there'll be no contracts signed above your head while I'm Kate Hervey's right and proper guardian, you can rest easy on that!"

The talk after that won't bear recounting! Such a

muddle things had been in, but now it all seemed to have sorted itself out. The beam on my face at not losing the Cottages was matched by the pleasure of Kate and Kathleen at having each other for next door neighbours. Best of all was the look on the face of my father, and the thought of the words he would be storing up to tell Father Jennet.

"Why didn't you tell us your name was Hervey?" I demanded. "We told everyone you were called Cooney!"

"You never asked my second name," she said, turning up her nose, "I could see no point at all in telling what I wasn't asked."

"You hardly talked at all," I said.

"And look where talk got you!" she exploded. "Look who talked about the bangle, and how we all nearly got killed because of it."

"What bangle is that, child?" asked Miss Cooney, curiously.

There was an awkward silence. I stole a glance at Kathleen, and she frowned at me, and nodded as if to say I must keep my mouth shut.

"An old one I brought with me," said Kate, sounding uncomfortable. "One of those men thought it was valuable, but it was just an old thing from home."

I opened my mouth to protest, for I didn't believe a word of it, but my father was quicker off the mark, and started telling Miss Cooney the tale of the catching of Dick and Jimmy, wasp stings all over them, as they tried to escape from the Point Field. The other two . . . unstung . . . had made a complete getaway. He went on and on about it, and I lost interest, for we already knew that story.

We had to wait till we three were alone again before we could ask Kate about it, and then she was quick to take offence.

"I did not steal it!" she said.

"Then why did you tell lies about it?"

"I . . . I . . . ."

"You did!"

"Well, only a little one," she said. "It wasn't mine. It wasn't anybody's really. I just found it."

"Where?" I asked, but inside me I knew the answer.

* * *

It was almost a week before we managed to find it, poking about in the charred ruins of Cooney's house. The bangle was scorched and dirty, but otherwise just the same.

"I don't want to touch it," Kathleen said.

"I think it is a lot of fuss about nothing," Kate said, putting it on her arm with a flourish. "There you are! I haven't turned black or gone up in a puff of smoke, have I? So much for bad luck!"

"You will take it back where you got it," I said. "You promised."

"If I must, I must," said Kate. "But I don't know why you are both so scared of an old bangle."

I could have told her, but I didn't bother. She was not of the Lanes, perhaps she would never understand. No one from the Lanes would have gone to Sleepers' Hill in the first time, no one would have moved the black stone, and found the steps which led down into the darkness there. No one . . .

"Take it back," I said. "It belongs to them."

"Who?"

"On the Hill," I said. "There will be no rest till it lies back where it came from."

"Oh nonsense," said Kate.

"Just put it back," I said.

And she did.

"I wasn't afraid of the bangle," Kathleen said.

"Neither was I," I replied.

"Just the same, I'm glad it has gone back."

"That is where it belongs," I said.

"Kate doesn't seem to feel it, does she?"

"Kate is a stranger," I said. "She had no call to fear anything she did not know about. It is our Hill, after all."

"Our Hill," said Kathleen.

Chapter Thirteen

I may own up now that there is not a true name in this story, but I'm not ashamed of it. That is the way it was agreed between the three of us, for the love of the Lanes and our own people. You would do the same for your own, no doubt . . . but you must judge that as I tell it. Whatever you decide, Kate and Kathleen made up my mind for me, sitting around the range in Cooney's cottage. They said they would not let me tell the tale if I would not promise to hide the place where it happened behind the names you know.

It was as simple as this: if I used the true names, men would be sent from Belfast to the Sleepers' Hill, and they would move the black stone by the tree and find the narrow entrance hidden there, and creep within the stone burying place.

It was Kate who found it, and she was the only one likely to, for no Lanes man would go near Sleepers' Hill. It was a holy place, an ancient place, a hidden place where the long men were laid to rest at the end of their days. The long men are gone now, their bodies dust; but their place remains.

Also available in Mammoth

EMER'S GHOST

Catherine Sefton

Who could possibly have imagined that an old and battered doll from a rubble-filled ditch could mean trouble and danger? Perhaps Emer should have listened more carefully to the fortune-teller; certainly a wooden doll who cries real tears is warning enough of something secret and strange. But it's only when Emer meets the doll's true owner that she realises she is being haunted . . . and that the doll, the ghost, and Emer herself are all part of the same dangerous mystery.

A Selected List of Fiction from Mammoth

While every effort is made to keep prices low, it is sometimes necessary to increase prices at short notice. Mammoth Books reserves the right to show new retail prices on covers which may differ from those previously advertised in the text or elsewhere.

The prices shown below were correct at the time of going to press.

☐	416 13972 8	**Why the Whales Came**	Michael Morpurgo	£2.50
☐	7497 0034 3	**My Friend Walter**	Michael Morpurgo	£2.50
☐	7497 0035 1	**The Animals of Farthing Wood**	Colin Dann	£2.99
☐	7497 0136 6	**I Am David**	Anne Holm	£2.50
☐	7497 0139 0	**Snow Spider**	Jenny Nimmo	£2.50
☐	7497 0140 4	**Emlyn's Moon**	Jenny Nimmo	£2.25
☐	7497 0344 X	**The Haunting**	Margaret Mahy	£2.25
☐	416 96850 3	**Catalogue of the Universe**	Margaret Mahy	£1.95
☐	7497 0051 3	**My Friend Flicka**	Mary O'Hara	£2.99
☐	7497 0079 3	**Thunderhead**	Mary O'Hara	£2.99
☐	7497 0219 2	**Green Grass of Wyoming**	Mary O'Hara	£2.99
☐	416 13722 9	**Rival Games**	Michael Hardcastle	£1.99
☐	416 13212 X	**Mascot**	Michael Hardcastle	£1.99
☐	7497 0126 9	**Half a Team**	Michael Hardcastle	£1.99
☐	416 08812 0	**The Whipping Boy**	Sid Fleischman	£1.99
☐	7497 0033 5	**The Lives of Christopher Chant**	Diana Wynne-Jones	£2.50
☐	7497 0164 1	**A Visit to Folly Castle**	Nina Beachcroft	£2.25

All these books are available at your bookshop or newsagent, or can be ordered direct from the publisher. Just tick the titles you want and fill in the form below.

Mandarin Paperbacks, Cash Sales Department, PO Box 11, Falmouth, Cornwall TR10 9EN.

Please send cheque or postal order, no currency, for purchase price quoted and allow the following for postage and packing:

UK   80p for the first book, 20p for each additional book ordered to a maximum charge of £2.00.

BFPO   80p for the first book, 20p for each additional book.

Overseas   £1.50 for the first book, £1.00 for the second and 30p for each additional book
including Eire   thereafter.

NAME (Block letters) ....

ADDRESS ....

....

....